Ruined

PERFECTLY IMPERFECT SERIES

secrets

NEVA ALTAJ

License notes

Copyright © 2022 Neva Altaj
www.neva-altaj.com

All rights reserved. No portion of this book may be reproduced in any form without permission from the publisher, except as permitted by U.S. copyright law.

This is a work of fiction. Names, characters, places, and incidents either are the product of the author's imagination or are used fictitiously. Any resemblance to actual persons, living or dead, events, or locales is entirely coincidental.

Editing by Susan Stradiotto (www.susanstradiotto.com)
Proofreading #1 by Beyond The Proof (www.beyondtheproof.ca)
Proofreading #2 by Yvette Rebello (yreditor.com)
Cover design by Deranged Doctor (www.derangeddoctordesign.com)
Paperback formatting by Stacey at Champagne Book Design

Author's Note

Dear reader, there are a few Italian words mentioned in the book, so here are the translations and clarifications:

Tesoro—treasure; endearment.

Stella mia—my star; endearment.

Piccola—little one, little girl; endearment.

Trigger Warning

Please be aware that this book contains content that some readers may find disturbing, such as gore, violence, and graphic descriptions of torture. There are also more steamy scenes than in the previous books in this series, and those include elements of mild BDSM, and the usage of toys.

RUINED

PERFECTLY IMPERFECT SERIES

secrets

Prologue

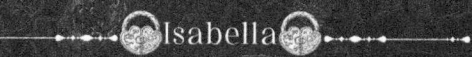
Isabella

Present
(Isabella 19 y.o.)

They shaved his hair.

I don't know why that detail hits me so hard.

Reaching for my husband's hand, I entwine our fingers and drop my forehead onto the mattress. I don't know what I hate more—the hospital smell, the beep of the machine next to the bed tracking his heartbeat, or how still he is.

Minutes pass. Maybe hours, I'm not sure.

I almost miss it—the tiny twitch of his fingers in my own. My head snaps up, and I find two dark brown eyes watching me.

"Oh, Luca..." I choke out, then lean over him and place a light, quick kiss on his lips.

He doesn't say anything, just keeps looking at me, probably wondering how I dared to kiss him, but I don't care. I was so scared for him, and I needed the stolen kiss to assure myself that he's alive.

I let go of his hand, sit up straighter in the chair, and wait for him to start giving me an earful. When he speaks, his voice is rough and deep, even deeper than usual, and the words that leave his mouth make me go ice-cold.

"Who are you?"

I stare at him.

Luca cocks his head to the side, regarding me with his intense, calculating gaze. I'm very familiar with this expression, because I'm usually on the receiving end of it when he's not happy with something I've done. But there is one huge difference this time. It's his eyes. The same eyes that I've hoped for so long would look at me with love instead of indifference. They are gazing at me now without a sliver of recognition.

"I'm Isabella," I whisper. "Your . . . wife."

He blinks, then looks away at the window on the other side of the room and takes a deep breath.

"So, Isabella," he says and turns to me. "Care to tell me who I am?

Part One

"Before"

Chapter one

Three Years Ago
(Isabella 16 y.o.)

"Isa!" Andrea yells my name as her loud footsteps pound up the stairs.

I turn in my chair to see my younger sister running into my room. She's only two years younger than me, but sometimes behaves like she's starting elementary rather than high school. By the time she reaches me, she's out of breath.

"You can't run through the house yelling." I point a pencil at her. "You're fourteen, not four."

"He's here!" She grabs my hand and starts dragging me out of the room, a face-splitting smile lighting up her eyes.

"Who?"

"Luca Rossi."

My heartbeat quickens, just like it does every time his name comes up, and I scurry after my sister, ignoring my own words of warning. We run down the hallway and the big stone staircase. As expected, we get several disapproving looks from the maid and two of my grandfather's men along the way, but I can't make myself think about etiquette now. He's here!

We dash through the front double doors and circle the house until we reach the big azalea bush on the back side, just a few yards from the French window outside my grandfather's study. Like we've done so many times before, I crouch behind it and pull Andrea down beside me. It's an ideal hiding spot, with a clear view into Nonno Giuseppe's office.

"I should have changed," I mumble, looking down at my cut-off jeans shorts and plain T-shirt. "I can't let Luca see me like this."

Andrea sizes me up and raises an eyebrow. "What's wrong with your clothes?"

"I look like a schoolgirl," I say, quickly removing my hair tie and combing my fingers through my hair. Mom says wearing my hair down adds a few years to my appearance.

"Oh?" Andrea chuckles. "Newsflash, Isa—you are."

"Well, I don't have to dress the part." I pout and look up at the window, waiting. "If I'd known Luca was coming over, I would've put on that beige dress."

The door to the study opens and Luca Rossi, one of my grandfather's capos, enters the room. I grab Andrea's hand and squeeze. I've been obsessing over him since I was six years old, when he jumped into the pool and saved my life after that idiot Enzo threw me in it. I don't remember ever being as scared as when my head dipped below the water, and my socked, fancy dress pulled me down. I wasn't a good swimmer, and I fruitlessly kicked my legs, trying to get to the surface. When I was sure I would die, two large hands suddenly grabbed me and pulled me up.

Never will I forget those smiling eyes as Luca carried me toward my hysterical mother. His expensive suit was dripping wet, and the strands of his long dark hair were plastered to his face. That evening, I told my mother that when I grew up, I would marry Luca Rossi. Maybe I fell in love with him that day.

"He's even hotter than last time I saw him." I sigh.

Luca has always been beautiful, and girls and women have often fallen over their own feet when he entered a room. It must have been his serious, slightly indifferent stance where other people were concerned, women included, that made him so interesting. He would walk into the room, do what he came for, and leave. No meaningless conversations. No lingering for gossip. If he had to stay longer for some event, because it was expected, he would either sit with my grandfather talking business, or lurk in one of the corners, observing the crowd. I loved watching him then, his huge body leaning on the wall, his dark eyes skimming over the room, observing everyone. Every sharp line of his perfect face has been carved into my brain. Over the years, however, his features have changed. His face matured, the lines becoming harsher and partially hidden with a short beard. His dark eyes have changed as well, getting a somehow harder, more sinister look in them. The only thing that has remained the same is his long, dark hair gathered in a bun on the top of his head. In our circle, it takes a certain kind of character for a man to wear his hair long and not be judged. But Luca Rossi has always been something else. Something *more* than other men.

"You're nuts." Andrea elbows me into my side, "He's double your age."

"I don't care."

"And he is married, Isa."

Pain pierces my heart at the mention of Simona, Luca's wife. Four years ago, I spent a week in bed, crying my eyes out, when I heard he was getting married. Although only twelve at the time, all I wanted was to be his wife one day. Like most girls, I dreamed about my wedding and in each of those childhood fantasies, it was always Luca standing next to me as my groom. People said Simona got pregnant on purpose to manipulate him into marriage, but it didn't make it hurt any less. I felt betrayed. He was mine!

I grab the branch in front of me and squeeze. "I hate that woman."

"I heard Aunt Agata telling Mama that she saw them fighting again," Andrea whispers, "in a restaurant full of people."

"About what?" I ask, without taking my eyes off Luca's handsome face.

"It sounded like they fought because Simona forgot to pick up Rosa from preschool." Andrea mumbles.

"How can a mother forget her child?" I stare disbelievingly at her. Even though Simona is a bitch, I didn't think she'd be capable of doing that.

"She was probably at one of her Botox appointments." My sister laughs.

I shake my head and turn back to watch Luca. He's sitting in a chair on the other side of my grandfather's desk, with his profile to us. Based on the grim expression on both of their faces, something serious is going on. I know my grandfather very well. When Giuseppe Agostini, the don of Chicago's Cosa Nostra Family, has that face on, it means nothing good is cooking. A scowl on Luca's face isn't new, though, but this time, it causes a lump to form in my throat. I haven't seen him smile in years, and he's been around the house a lot since becoming a capo.

"I'm going back." I brush away a stray tear and turn to leave.

Every time I see him, it gets harder. It's as if a weight settles over my chest. I know he'll never be with me. And still, I can't make myself stay away. Andrea calls me crazy for obsessing over someone so much older. Maybe I am. But I can't help it. It started as hero-worshipping when he saved my life. In the last couple of years, however, that child adoration has transformed into something else entirely.

"Don't be sad, Isa." Andrea wraps her arm around my waist. "There are other men who'd worship the ground you walk on. You are the granddaughter to the don of the Cosa Nostra. When the time comes for you to marry, there will be a line of suitors waiting here for you. Someone will come by, sweep you off your feet, and you'll forget all about Luca Rossi. It's just a teenage crush."

"Yeah." I nod and put a fake smile on my face, the one I've been practicing with Mom. "You're right. Let's go back."

One year ago
(Isabella 18 y.o.)

The crowd is scattered around the garden, drinking and laughing. My grandfather must have invited everyone in the Chicago area with Italian blood to my birthday party.

"That waiter is super cute." Catalina, my best friend,

nudges me with her elbow. "I think I'm going to grab another piece of cake and check him out a bit better. You want to tag along?"

"Nope, I'm good," I say.

"But, look at him! He's got dimples when he laughs."

I glance over at the man standing next to the food table, conversing with one of the guests. He's in his early twenties, with short blond hair and a really nice smile.

"You go." I nod toward the cutie who's captured her interest. "I'll wait for you here."

Catalina giggles, winks at me, and rushes to the tables laden with food. She approaches the cute waiter and starts to flirt, and for a moment, I wish I were able to do the same. Too bad I only have eyes for one man.

I look toward the opposite side of the garden where Luca is sitting with my grandfather and Lorenzo Barbini, my nonno's underboss. They seem to be discussing business, not really paying too much attention to the festive atmosphere around them. Luca hasn't even glanced my way since he got here, which is nothing new.

It wasn't always like this. When I was little, I'd run across the lawn the moment I saw him arrive. He would catch and spin me around when I jumped into his arms, making me squeal in delight. But he stopped doing that the summer I turned thirteen.

I remember that day as if it happened yesterday. The moment I saw him exiting his car, I dashed outside and ran across the driveway to him. He didn't open his arms to catch me that day. Instead, he just brushed his hand down my hair and went inside the house. That's all I got during his next few visits—a light brush of my hair. I guess he decided I was too old for spinning around, or maybe that it wasn't proper. Then, even those light stokes of my hair stopped. In the last few years, I was left with simply watching him from a distance.

Like now.

"Isabella!"

I throw a look over my shoulder to find Enzo, Catalina's idiot cousin, barreling in my direction.

"Shit," I murmur and turn around, intending to head inside the house. Before I can make my escape, he comes around and steps into my path.

"So beautiful." He wraps his hand around my wrist and bends his head to rest on mine, inhaling as he does so. "And smelling like flowers."

"Leave me alone, Enzo." I try to wriggle free, but his grip is strong, and he pulls me tighter.

"Oh, come on, Isa! Why are you always acting like an iceberg?"

"Enzo! You're drunk!" I look around, searching for Andrea or anyone else who could get me away from him. There are dozens of guests milling across the garden, but no one is close enough to come to my aid. I could yell, but I don't want to make a scene because there are too many important people here tonight.

"Of course, I am." He laughs. "It's your eighteenth birthday. It's only natural to drink to that, yeah? Come on, let me give you a birthday kiss."

"Get away from me." I sneer and try to wiggle away again.

"But it's just one kiss. Come on, Isa, don't be such a—"

He stops midsentence, his eyes focusing on something behind me, then he tilts his head up until his gaze stops well above my own. The color in his face starts rapidly draining. A hand adorned with a thin, white gold wedding band reaches from behind me and wraps around Enzo's wrist in a vice-like grip. Enzo lets go of me, but the newcomer's long, strong fingers squeeze the idiot's wrist tighter until he whimpers. I don't pay attention to Enzo. My heartbeat picks up as I stare at the two bracelets encircling the other person's wrist. One is a wide silver cuff and the other a black leather band. I bought both with my pocket money five years ago and gave them to him. I didn't know he actually wore them.

I take a deep breath, trying to keep my racing heart from exploding as I move my eyes from the bracelets back to the wedding band on his finger. Something dies in me again, just like the first time I saw the ring on his hand.

"Touch her again," Luca's smooth, whiskey-like voice says above me, "and you die."

Enzo nods maniacally and whimpers again. "Yes, Mr. Rossi."

"Get lost," Luca barks and releases Enzo's hand.

I stare at Enzo's back as he runs toward the gate. I don't dare face my savior. If I do, I might fall apart. Until this morning, I still believed there might be a small chance I would get to be with Luca someday. That sliver of hope evaporated the moment my father informed me that he agreed to give my hand in marriage to Angelo Scardoni, the youngest of my grandfather's capos, when I turn twenty-one. I always knew I would end up in an arranged marriage because it was the only option for the Cosa Nostra don's granddaughter, but I still hoped.

"Everything okay, tesoro?"

"Yes." I nod, keeping my eyes fixed on the gate. "Thank you, Luca."

"If he pesters you again, let me know."

"I will."

"Okay." There's a slight touch at the back of my head as if he lightly brushed my hair. "Happy birthday, Isabella."

I wait until I no longer feel Luca behind me, then turn around slowly and watch him as he walks away, leaving me to stand with an overload of emotions brewing within, with nowhere to go. Something squeezes in my chest. I wonder how it would feel to have him walking toward me for once. Maybe start a meaningless conversation, even if it's only in passing. This is the most we've spoken to each other in the past two years. I've often feared he's forgotten I exist.

I hear my name being called and turn to see Catalina waving at me to come over. Throwing one last look at Luca's retreating form over my shoulder, I head toward the tables with food, running my fingers along my hair where his hand brushed it.

Chapter Two

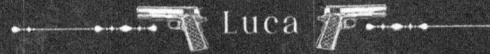

Three months ago
(Luca 35 y.o.)

I LEAN MY ELBOWS ON THE STEERING WHEEL AND WATCH the video playing on my phone.

A pair of black pants and a red dress, obviously discarded in a hurry, are lying on the floor in the middle of the room. A man in a white shirt is sitting at the edge of the bed, while a blonde-haired woman is kneeling between his legs, sucking his dick. The room they are in is . . . my bedroom. And the woman who's currently choking on her bodyguard's dick is my dear wife.

I put the phone in my jacket, take my gun from the glove compartment, and leave the car.

It's half past one in the morning, and there's no one in the hall. My footsteps echo off the dark marble floor and up the wide stairwell. When I reach the third floor, I turn right and walk down the hallway to my daughter's room to make sure she's not home. Rosa is having a sleepover at her friend's, as she usually does when I have to leave home for a couple of days for work. She and her mother never got along well.

I open the door to Rosa's room and peek inside. Empty. I close the door, then continue to the other end of the hallway, toward my bedroom.

Simona is still on her knees in front of the bodyguard when I enter. The lamp in the corner is giving off more than enough light for me to clearly see the man's flushed face above Simona's bobbing head. I lift my gun, aiming at the center of his forehead, and pull the trigger. The loud bang makes the nightstand rattle, and blood sprays all over the white, satin sheets. Simona screams, then jumps up and away from the body now sprawled across the bed. Her face and hair also bear red splotches, and there are some on her breasts and neck. Seems like some of her lover's brain matter ended up in her hair as well. She is still wailing when I walk casually over to her and grab her upper arm.

"Let me go!" she yells as I drag her out of the room and down the hallway. "You killed him, you monster!"

Simona keeps shrieking all the way down the two flights of stairs, trying to squirm out of my grasp. I ignore her protests and head toward the wide-open front door. Two of my security guards run inside, but stop at the entrance, their eyes bulging out upon seeing us. A maid comes out around the corner from the hall where staff have their rooms and freezes midstep. She's clutching her knitted cardigan around herself with her gaze locked on Simona's naked and blood-splattered body. I pass the guards and drag my screaming wife outside, and down the four stone steps to the driveway.

"You'll receive the divorce papers in the morning," I spit out and release her arm.

"What? Luca, please! It was a mistake." She reaches over as if to take my hand.

"Don't you dare fucking touch me! Get the fuck out of my house."

"You can't do this!" she wails. "Luca!"

I turn and go back inside. For some reason, I'm not even angry. The only thing I feel is disgust. With her, but also with myself for not ending things with the bitch sooner.

"Send a maid to bring her something to put on, and call a taxi," I tell Marco, who is standing by the door. "She's not to come inside the house."

"Of course, Mr. Rossi." He nods quickly.

"There is a body in my bedroom. Have someone take care of that, too," I say as I move toward the stairwell. I'm halfway to the second floor when my brother's voice reaches me.

"Luca? What's going on?"

Damian is standing on the landing to the second floor, wearing only his boxer briefs. Behind him is a dark-haired girl wrapped in a blanket, peeking over his shoulder.

"Simona and I decided to split," I say as I'm climbing the stairwell. "She's leaving."

"Naked?"

"Yes." I stop in front of him and cast a glance at the girl cowering behind his back. "Good evening, Arianna."

"Hi, Luca." She smiles nervously.

"Does your father know where you're spending the night?"

"Nope," she mumbles.

I shake my head and look back at my brother. "Franco is going to kill you."

"Arianna is twenty-one. I think she can make her own decisions, Luca." He smirks.

"She's also engaged," I say and keep heading up the stairs. "I'm going to crash. I have a meeting at eight tomorrow."

"Luca?" he calls after me. "Was that a gunshot we heard earlier?"

"Yes."

"Care to elaborate?"

"Nope. Go back to bed, Damian."

When I reach the third floor, I drop by my bedroom to collect the phone charger and a change of clothes for tomorrow, then head into Rosa's room to sleep.

Chapter Three

Two months ago
(Isabella 19 y.o.)

I SIT AT THE EDGE OF THE BED AND TAKE MY GRANDFATHER'S frail hand in mine. I'm trying to be careful not to nudge the attached IV, supplying fluids to keep him hydrated. I gently rearrange the tube and move the pole so I don't accidentally bump it with my knees. The nightstand on the left is covered with all sorts of medicine bottles. At least ten of them. The air in the room feels stale, permeated with the smell of pharmaceuticals that seems to cling to everything.

"Nonno," I whisper. His cheeks are sunken, and there are big black circles around his eyes. He looks really bad. "How are you feeling?"

"Like I've been hit by a train."

"You had a heart attack. It's to be expected. You'll get better in a few days."

He smiles sadly. "We both know that's not true." I start

to say something, but he squeezes my hand and continues, "We need to talk. It's important."

"It can wait until you're feeling better."

"No, it can't wait." He shakes his head. "When I'm gone, there will be chaos. You know that."

"You are not dying anytime soon. The Family needs you." I press my lips together tightly. "I need you."

Giuseppe Agostini has been leading the Chicago branch of the Cosa Nostra Family for twenty years, but he's also been the rock of our own family. While he had his own wing, we all lived in the same house. I can't imagine not having him here.

"It's the circle of life. The old are meant to go, and the young stay."

"You're sixty-nine. That's not old."

"I know, stella mia. But, it is what it is." He sighs and squeezes my hand. "You know how things work in our world. If a don dies without a successor defined, there will be an internal war within the Family. I called the capos to come the day after tomorrow, so I can name my replacement."

I don't understand why he's telling me this. He's not dying. It was just a minor heart attack. People live for years after that happens.

"The man I plan to name will need the connection to our family to ensure no one will confront him and make matters worse," he continues, "Do you understand what I'm saying, Isabella?"

"No, I don't think so."

"We need to tie our families together. By marriage."

Things finally start to make sense and chills run down my spine. "You want me to marry? Right away?"

"Yes. Will you do that, Isi?"

Tears start to gather in the corners of my eyes. He's the only one who ever calls me that.

"Did you talk with Angelo already?" I ask.

I have nothing against Angelo. He's a nice guy, and we've been on a few dates, but I never felt anything for him, not even a spark. And I hoped I'd get a few more years of freedom.

"Yes." He nods. "I told him that the engagement is off."

"Off?" I blink. "I don't understand."

"Angelo is a good kid, but he's too young to be a don, Isi. The rest of the Family would never stand by him."

I draw my brows together, confused. "Who am I marrying then?"

"The only man who can take over all the shit I'm going to throw at him and not crumble under the weight of it."

My breathing becomes shallow, and my heart starts thumping so hard I'm afraid it's going to burst out of my chest.

"You're marrying Luca Rossi," my grandfather says the words I've been longing to hear for more than a decade, and I can only stare at him.

"But . . . he's already married," I say, dumbfounded.

"He and Simona are divorcing. It should be done in a matter of days. I know you're only nineteen, and he is so much older than you . . ."

I shake my head and bend down to wrap my arms around his frail form. "I will gladly marry Luca, Nonno."

 Luca

I knock on the door of Don Agostini's study.

"Come in," a faint voice calls from the inside.

The Family has known for quite some time that Giuseppe hasn't been well. I've been meeting with him at least once a week to update him on the real estate business, so I've witnessed the deterioration firsthand. Still, the sight that greets me makes me falter. He looks as if he's aged twenty years since the last time I saw him.

"Luca." He nods toward the chair on the other side of the desk. "Please sit."

"How are you feeling, Boss?" I ask as I take a seat.

"Awful, as you can see." He smiles. "I'll be short because Lorenzo and the other capos are coming in less than an hour."

I've been wondering what he wants to talk about since I got his call yesterday. At first, I assumed it would be business, as usual. But if that's the case, it could be discussed after the meeting with the capos.

"I had a heart attack two days ago," he says. "It was a minor thing, but as the doctor so nicely put it to me, I need to start getting my things in order. Fast."

"All right. How can I help?"

"By taking over."

"Okay." I nod.

Giuseppe has been giving me more responsibilities over the last two years. He's also transferred the real estate dealings to me completely, saying he couldn't handle everything. I guess he plans to delegate another part of the business. "What do you need me to take over?"

"The Chicago Family of Cosa Nostra, Luca."

I stare at him. Saying that he caught me by surprise would be an understatement. Everyone expected the next don to be Lorenzo Barbini.

"What about Lorenzo?" I ask.

"Lorenzo is a good underboss. He's been organizing and overseeing the operations well so far," Giuseppe says. "However, he's not capable of making decisions that have the Family's best interests in mind instead of his own. I always planned for it to be you."

"Well, some warning in advance would have been appreciated."

"Consider yourself warned."

"Is that why you called all the capos today?" I ask.

"Yes, one of the reasons."

"And the others?"

"Just one more. I'm moving up the timeline on an important matter." He pauses, eyes locked onto mine. Despite his frail appearance, his gaze remains steady and scrutinizing. What is he hoping to find? "Isabella's upcoming marriage," he continues after bit.

"To Angelo Scardoni?"

A smile pulls across his face. "To you."

I close my eyes, then open them widely. They said it was his heart, not his brain, that was going bad. "Isabella is nineteen," I say. "I'm not marrying a child."

"She's not a child. Her mother married at eighteen. I don't see a problem."

"Well, I do. I could be her father, technically."

"You're not even thirty."

"I'm thirty-five." And he knows that very well, but he just waves his hand through the air like it's nothing of importance.

"Isabella is a good girl, maybe a little stubborn sometimes, but she's extremely clever and very well versed in social interaction and Family affairs. Not to mention exceptionally beautiful."

That she is. I've seen her quite often, and I can't deny the obvious. With her long chestnut hair falling down her back in soft curls, a pert nose, and huge dark eyes that are almost too big for her face, she is stunning. She isn't very tall, but she has an amazing little body, a ridiculously tiny waist, and the most perfect ass I've ever seen. And the fact that I've noticed a nineteen-year-old's ass at all is all kinds of fucked up. I've also known Isabella since she was a kid, and the idea of marrying her sounds completely insane.

It seems that Giuseppe doesn't catch my reluctance because he continues speaking. "She'll be a good wife to you. And if you let her, a good partner."

"Partner in what?"

"In life, Luca. When you're in a position of power, a wife you can lean on and trust is indispensable. For men like us, it's rare to find a partner with whom you can share the good, as well as the bad. And there will be a shitload of bad, trust me."

I shake my head. Who would have thought the don would be romantic. "The only person one can truly trust is themselves, Boss. And, sometimes, his closest blood kin. I've learned that lesson well."

"Not all women are like Simona." He reaches with his hand to take a glass of water from the desk, and I can't help but notice the way his fingers are shaking. "What happened between you two? I know you never got along well, but a divorce?"

I recline back in the chair and cross my arms in front of me. "I caught her giving her bodyguard a blow job. In our bed. I suspected it for quite some time, so I set up a camera in the room."

"Christ. Is he alive?"

"Nope. And she barely escaped the same fate."

"I wondered why she went along with the divorce so easily. How's Rosa dealing with the situation?" he asks after a pause.

"Simona was never interested in her. Rosa was only a means to an end. A tool to make me marry her."

"I'm sorry. I hope Isabella will get along well with your daughter."

"So you're serious about the marriage thing?"

With his head bowed slightly, the don looks at me over the rims of his glasses. He opens a drawer, takes out a stack of papers, and throws them onto the desk in front of me. A marriage agreement. I can't believe I just managed to get rid of one wife, and he's saddling me with a child bride before my divorce is even finalized.

"What am I going to do with a nineteen-year-old, Boss?"

"Whatever you do, you will do it with respect. Isabella might be young, but she's still my granddaughter, and a person who will help secure your place as the new don. Keep that in mind."

I stare at the stack of papers in front of me. Clenching my teeth together, I give him my resigned nod.

Chapter
four

 Isabella

IS IT POSSIBLE FOR THE SAME DAY TO BE THE HAPPIEST and the saddest of my life?

I tilt my head and regard my reflection in the mirror while standing on a small stool as two seamstresses kneel on the floor, adjusting the length of my wedding gown. There wasn't enough time to order a custom dress, so my mother took me to the most prestigious wedding salon in the city and picked the most expensive dress available. It had to be adjusted to fit my rather impressive behind.

Andrea and I were similarly built when we were younger, but when puberty hit, my sister kept her slender figure and I didn't. It's as if my body is made of two halves that don't really fit together. I love my narrow waist and flat stomach. My breasts are average but firm. Having a petite upper body allows me to purchase the smallest size T-shirts and tops. The bottom half of me, however, is a different story all together. My ass and hips are at least two sizes too big for my torso. Diets never helped much because they only caused my breasts and my already thin arms to get smaller before my ass would get the memo.

Andrea is always telling me I'm crazy and she'd kill for a butt like mine, but I don't see it. Although I've never struggled with any self-esteem problems, I wouldn't say no to a smaller booty and slimmer thighs. I sigh as I look at my reflection again.

"What do you want to be done with your hair, Miss Isabella?" the hairstylist asks.

"Leave it loose," my mother suggests from the chair in the corner of the room. She's been overseeing the preparations since five this morning.

"Loose is okay." I shrug.

Luca didn't come to see me. Not on the day my grandfather announced that we'll be getting married, and not any time during the following weeks. I guess he considered it not necessary since we already knew each other.

I assess my reflection again, noting the long, white, lacy dress and expensive tiara on top of my head. My dream is finally coming true. But, I never thought it would be such a bitter experience. Based on what I overheard the morning I eavesdropped outside of my grandfather's study, I should have expected it.

"What am I going to do with a nineteen-year-old," Luca said. As if I was a stray dog someone brought in off the street. One he couldn't throw out, but he didn't want there either.

I'm glad I only overheard the tail end of the conversation. God knows what else he said before that.

There is a knock on the door and my father's head peeks

inside. "You're beautiful, Isa." He smiles and turns to my mother. "Emma, we need to hurry or we're going to be late."

"We'll be down in a minute," she says, moving somewhere behind me.

The staff leave the room first, my mother following, then Andrea and I exit last.

"Smile, Isa! You're finally marrying Luca," she whispers. "It still feels surreal."

"Yeah."

"Oh, come on. It's your wedding day for God's sake. I expected you to be ecstatic. People will expect you to be happy."

"I'm just nervous," I lie. I haven't told her about what I heard Luca say in Grandfather's study. "Here, better?" I ask and offer one of my favorite fake smiles.

"Perfect. I love that one, I've never really managed to pull off the right mix of happiness with a tiny bit of shyness. You were always Mom's best student." She laughs.

Yes, it's all about appearances in our world.

Luca

My divorce is official as of yesterday afternoon. And now, not even twenty-four hours later, I'm standing in front of an altar, waiting for my new bride. Unbelievable.

The church's tall door opens, and Isabella, on her father's arm, steps inside. I take the opportunity to study my future wife as she approaches. Maybe it's the light, but her face looks different from the last time I saw her for more than a fleeting second. She's still breathtaking. Still the same long hair, huge eyes, and sharp cheekbones. I can't pinpoint exactly what it is, but there's something amiss. She gives the impression that she's happy. A small smile is on her lips, and her head is held high—a picture-perfect image of a radiant bride. I move my gaze back to her eyes, and that's when I see it. Her face might be showing happiness and joy, but the emotion doesn't reach her eyes. Instead, they seem . . . empty.

She takes the final step to stand beside me, her gaze focused solely on the priest. Of course she doesn't want this either. What nineteen-year-old would want to be tied to a man almost twice her age? She must be scared about what's happening. I should have gone to speak with her beforehand, met her properly prior to the wedding. It's not as if I'm planning on us having a marriage that fits the true sense of the word, but still.

As the priest starts speaking, I reach out to take her hand in mine, and hear her sharp intake of breath. Isabella looks down at our joined hands, then lifts her gaze to stare right at me. Her eyes are not vacant anymore, and as she watches me, I can almost see the fire burning in their dark depths. I like that much better than the dead look.

After the priest finishes and we exchange rings, I lean down and place a quick kiss on her cheek. When I straighten and look at her, I find her watching me with that empty stare again.

I lift my glass and sip the seltzer without taking my eyes off the corner of the room where my young wife is standing with her sister and mother.

The moment we arrived at the country club, where the wedding lunch is being held, Isabella left my side and went to the opposite end of the room. She hasn't looked in my direction once. I should be relieved. Instead, I've been watching her for more than an hour, noticing every man who gives her a passing glance. It pisses me off. Not only the looks other men are giving her, but also the fact that it's bothering me.

"What an unexpected turn of events," Lorenzo Barbini says as he steps up next to me.

"Oh?" I take another sip of my drink. "Do you mean the wedding or the fact that Giuseppe named me his successor?"

"Both, to be honest. I thought the plan was to have Angelo Scardoni marry his granddaughter."

"Plans change," I say.

Lorenzo has been Giuseppe's underboss for almost fifteen years, which is longer than I've been a capo. It's understandable that he was surprised by the don's decision. Everyone was, including me. Usually, when a don dies or decides to step down, it's his son or son-in-law who takes over the leadership. If that's not the case, then the reigns are passed to the underboss. My new grandfather-in-law chose to forge a new path.

"Are you sure you can handle everything your new position will entail?" he asks.

I've never aspired to lead the Family. Making arms deals, managing transactions so everything runs smoothly, and bringing in money was my main focus. Presently, the operations I oversee account for more than fifty percent of our earnings.

"Do you think you'd make a better don?" I ask.

"Let's be real here, Luca. You're a businessman and you do a great job. But you rarely attend Family events, and I'm pretty sure you have no idea how to handle internal affairs."

He's right. I don't give a damn about their dinners, or who banged whose wife. Assuming the head position of the Chicago Cosa Nostra means resolving a bunch of private matters, meddling in debt issues between high-level members, and arranging marriages within the Family. Other people's personal drama is not something I enjoy. But how little I care about the social aspect of the job doesn't mean I'll allow anyone to question my abilities.

"Yes, I assume you'd be better versed in handling that part, considering that sitting at parties is all you've been doing recently. Tell me, Lorenzo, would you run the Family the same way you're running our casinos? Because from what I know, you've been dealing with significant losses for months." I smile, enjoying the shock that spreads over his face. "Losses, might I add, that were covered with the profits I brought in from the gun deals. Maybe you should focus on taking care of your own shit before you aspire to take on more responsibilities?"

"He who flies high, falls deep," Lorenzo mumbles into his glass.

I smile and grab the knot of his tie, pulling him up slightly. "I didn't hear you well." I bend, getting into his face, "Can you please repeat that?"

Lorenzo's nostrils flare as the redness starts spreading

over his face. He stares at me with bulging eyes for a few moments, then grits his teeth.

"I said, your information is wrong," he sneers, "There is nothing wrong with the casino business."

"Oh. My bad, then." I release his tie and nod toward the corner of the room. "Seems like your wife is looking for you."

Lorenzo gives me one angry stare, then marches away, and I turn my eyes back to my young wife. Franco Conti, the capo in charge of laundering money, is speaking with Emma, Isabella's mother. I haven't collaborated with Franco much, since he only handles money that comes from our casinos. Damian is in charge of laundering what my operations make, and I plan on keeping it that way. Standing next to Franco is Dario D'Angelo, the oldest son of Capo Santino D'Angelo, talking with Isabella. She smiles at something he says, then turns toward her sister, and I notice the way Dario's gaze passes down her body while she's not looking. Grinding my teeth, I pivot around and head to the bar. Who she talks to shouldn't concern me. I'm halfway to my destination when I hear female laughter ring out behind me, so I peer over my shoulder. Isabella and her sister are giggling at something Dario has just said.

It shouldn't bother me that another man can make her laugh. But it does. It's like a damn itch in my side. I ignore the urge to walk over and shoo Santino's son away from Isabella. Instead, I join Orlando Lombardi, another capo who handles the Family's gambling business, at the bar.

"Did you hear about last week's shitstorm in New York?" he asks when I take a seat next to him.

"I'm not into gossip." I motion for the barman to bring me another seltzer. "Too much shit to deal with here."

"Ajello annihilated two Camorra clans in one night. Forty-seven people. Looks like they tried sticking their fingers in his business." Orlando leans close to me. "One of my nieces is married to a guy who works as a foot soldier for Ajello. She heard Ajello was shot during the skirmish."

I take a sip of my drink. What the don of New York does doesn't concern me in the least, I have no business with him. But I can't say I'm not a bit curious. That man has always been a mystery. "Is he dead?"

"No. But that's all I know," Orlando says. "His ranks are too tightly stitched, and his men are loyal to a point of madness. My niece only overheard the conversation when her husband talked over the phone with someone."

I'm trying my best to keep my eyes focused on my drink, but can't fight the compulsion to take another look at Isabella. When I do, I find her watching me. The moment our gazes connect, however, she turns back to Dario.

"You know, I sometimes think that man doesn't exist," Orlando continues. "How come no one has ever met him?"

"Giuseppe did," I say and glance at my wife again. She's still talking with the idiot. "Last year."

"No! Why did he never mention it?"

"Because Giuseppe doesn't need to share what he does with anyone."

"He told you," he says with an envious glint in his eyes. "What was the meeting about?"

"One of our soldiers went to New York to visit a girlfriend who was there for work. And he didn't ask permission to enter Ajello's territory. Giuseppe met with Ajello to resolve the issue."

"And did they? Resolve the issue?"

"Yes." I nod but keep one eye on Isabella.

"Ajello released the guy?"

"In a way," I say. "He sent back his head via FedEx."

"Jesus fuck."

Santino's kid is still standing with Isabella. I lower my glass to the bar and stand up. "I'm off."

"Leaving in the middle of your own wedding reception?"

"I have a meeting with Sergei Belov this afternoon."

He widens his eyes at me. "I didn't know you were doing business with the Bratva."

"Well, we already established that you don't know that many things, Orlando."

I leave Orlando staring daggers at my back and head to collect my wife.

Isabella

I stare out the window of the limousine, watching the buildings as we pass them by, and try to smother the need to turn and face Luca. He made sure he sat as far away from me as possible, on the other side of the back seat. We've been driving for almost an hour, and he hasn't said a word to me. Instead, he's been engrossed by typing something on his phone.

My thoughts fly back to the church and our wedding this morning. I was so damn excited when the priest said "You may kiss the bride". It's not that I expected Luca to devour me in front of all those people, but I did want a real kiss. And what did I get? A light peck on the cheek. Next, he might as well have taken out candy from his pocket and given it to me. It hurts, the way he's acting.

I sigh and continue looking outside, wondering what the hell I should do now. Just say *who cares* and see where this situation leads us? Live with a husband who remains a stranger because we ignore each other? Nope, I won't allow it. My self-pity party ends here. I finally married a man whom I've secretly loved for years, and I'll be damned if I let him sweep me under the carpet. Luca may not care about me now, but I will make him fall in love with me, or I'll die trying.

He has a problem with our age difference. I clearly heard him say that. Well, I can't do anything about how old I am, so it's one of the obstacles I'll need to overcome. I guess I'll have to give him a wake-up call. I may be young, but I know what I want. Him. Loving me. And I'm ready to fight for it.

The limo stops in front of a big white mansion, and Luca exits and comes around to open my door. Gathering my skirt, I take his extended hand, and get out to regard my new home. It's smaller than my grandfather's house, where I grew up, but still huge.

"Take Mrs. Rossi's suitcase upstairs," he says to the driver and motions for me to follow him inside. "I suppose you'll want to change and rest, so I'll take you to your room. Damian will show you around the house before dinner."

"Your brother?" I ask as we enter the big foyer.

"Yes. I have work to do."

"Oh?" I might be in love with him, but it doesn't mean I'll allow him to treat me like a doormat. "I don't remember marrying your brother, Luca."

He stops in his tracks and turns to me. "What does that mean?"

"It means that you will be the one to show me the house and introduce me to your staff," I say in a cold voice and enjoy the way his eyes widen in disbelief. Didn't expect me to have a backbone, did he? Well, surprise. "Where's your daughter?"

"Rosa is at her friend's house. She'll be home for dinner."

"Good. Please take me to my room now."

Luca cocks his head to the side, eyeing me with interest, then heads to the big stairway as I lag a few paces behind. I always admired the way he walks. His stride is slow, like a wolf on the prowl. Letting my eyes travel up his body, I check out his long legs and broad shoulders, and stop at the top of his head where his hair is gathered in a bun.

So many times, I've daydreamed about taking out that hair tie and threading my fingers through those black strands. I wonder how long his hair is now. The only time I saw it loose was after he jumped into the pool to save me all those years ago. His bun must have come undone in the process, spilling his mane free. It was shoulder-length back then.

I remember everything about him. Observing Luca in secret was all I ever could do, so I made sure to catch every single detail and store it in my mental vault, labeled with his name. The way his body changed over the years, becoming brawny, harder. Since I turned sixteen, I imagined that huge body wrapped around mine, holding me tight. Loving me.

I was seventeen the first time I pleasured myself, and I did it by imagining it was his hand between my legs instead of mine. From that day on, I've been doing it every single night before going to sleep. Sometimes even during the day. Whenever I've felt lonely or sad, I would lock myself in my room, get under the blanket, and imagine Luca lying next to me while I orgasmed. If people knew, they may think I'm silly for being in love with a man without actually knowing him that well. I don't care.

When we reach the third floor, Luca nods toward the door on the left and opens it. "My room," he says.

I take a glance, noticing an enormous bed under the window. Most of the furniture is made of dark wood that works well with the pale beige walls and curtains in the same shade.

"This room is not used," he says, opening the next door. The room seems the same size as his, but the furniture here is mostly white, with curtains and a rug in a soft peach color. There's a connecting door on the left wall that probably leads to his bedroom. He quickly shuts the door and ushers me down the corridor until we reach the last two rooms.

"Rosa's room." He nods to the one on the left with a big "Do Not Disturb" sticker on it, then turns to the door on the right and opens it. "This is you."

It's a nice space. Big, with several tall windows and light wood furniture. My suitcase stands in the middle of the carpet next to a big fluffy sofa.

"I'll come by at six to take you downstairs to have dinner," he says and leaves.

I look around one more time. So, he placed me as far from him as possible on this floor. It won't do. I walk to my suitcase and grab the handle. Rolling it in front of me so my dress doesn't catch within the wheels, I leave the room and head toward the other end of the corridor. Luca is just entering his room when he hears me coming. He takes a step back and watches me approach.

"Something wrong with your room?" he asks.

I stop in front of the room adjacent to his and tilt my chin up. His hooded eyes are peering at me, glaring with expression that I can't quite read.

"Not at all," I say, roll my suitcase inside and close the door behind me.

Luca

I look at the door that connects my bedroom to the room Isabella has claimed and listen to the sounds coming from the other side. There is no way she's staying that close to me. I'll let it be for now, but first thing in the morning, she's going back to the room across from Rosa's. I hear her move around, and then the water turns on in her ensuite bathroom. My teenage wife is taking a shower just a few yards from me, and suddenly, my mind conjures up images of her perfect little body under the spray.

I shake my head. What the fuck is wrong with me? I'm imagining having sex with a teenager. And one that's probably never slept with a man before. Jesus. I march out of the room and slam the door shut behind me as if it'll help erase the images of Isabella naked and wet. Or the temptation to pin her body between mine and the tiles of the shower wall while holding her wrists above her head.

It's quarter to six when I get back from the meeting with Sergei Belov. One of my weapons suppliers got a hold of several crates of military-issued crossbows, but no one knew how they worked. Belov was the only person who came to mind that might know how to handle that shit. Based on his grinning face when I showed him the sample, he had plenty of experience with them. Somehow, I wasn't surprised. But he did stun me when he asked if I could get him a tank. Then, he shrugged and said, "Asking for a friend." They must have more than one lunatic in the Bratva.

I climb the stairs to the third floor and knock on the door of Isabella's temporary room. She opens and looks me over, focusing on my jeans and black shirt. I notice a glint of astonishment in her eyes.

"No dressing up for dinner here?" she asks as we head toward the stairway.

"I hate suits."

Isabella's eyebrows lift in surprise. Wordlessly, she descends the stairs in front of me, giving me an unobstructed view of her behind. A pink sleeveless top that ties around her neck is molded to her torso and narrow waist, and it only emphasizes her perky round ass, clad in tight black trousers. It takes tremendous willpower to move my eyes away from it.

When we get to the ground floor, she stops in front of the staff lined up on the right side of the foyer.

"This is Isabella. My wife," I say and introduce them one by one, starting with the housekeeper, then the maids, two drivers, the gardener, and finally the kitchen staff.

With that done, I turn to the other side where my security people stand and introduce them, as well. I don't expect her to remember any of their names because there are more than thirty people that work here.

"This is the second shift," I tell her. "I'll introduce you to the first shift when they arrive in the morning."

"Thank you." She nods and follows me to the dining room that spans a quarter of the ground floor on the east side.

I remember the first time I brought Simona here after we were married at the city hall. She was overwhelmed with the number of security guards and the size of the house itself, and she jumped and squealed when anyone carrying a firearm passed by her. Isabella, on the contrary, takes all of this in without batting an eye. I guess it's nothing new to her. She was raised in a house twice the size of mine and with significantly more armed guards.

Damian is already in the dining room, sitting at the table to the left of the head seat. He sees us come in and stands up, extending his hand.

"Finally." He laughs. "I started wondering if Luca decided to hide you in your room forever."

"Isabella, this is my brother," I say and watch closely for her reaction.

My brother is twelve years younger than me and, as women like to call him, "drop-dead gorgeous." People usually focus on his blue eyes, styled hair, and impeccable clothing, while underestimating him in the process, thinking him as a playboy. He does his best to uphold that impression with his behavior. Not many people know what a genius is hiding under that expensive haircut. Damian has a knack when it comes to numbers and the real estate market. Because of that, he handles the finances of my business dealings. He also launders millions of dollars on a monthly basis.

"Just Isa, please," my wife says.

"I have to say, I couldn't think of a name that would fit you better, Isa." He smiles at her. "Bella."

I shake my head. He's already turned on the charm.

"No flirting, Damian. Where's Rosa?"

"She said she'll eat in her room."

I turn to the maid waiting close by. "Get my daughter down here. Right now."

As we sit at the table waiting for Rosa, I lean back in my chair and observe as Isabella and Damian discuss how she likes the house. They clearly hit it off right from the start, which I expected since they're close in age. I wonder if she'll try seducing him like Simona did.

"You weren't at the wedding," Isabella says.

Damian smiles. "Yeah, I try to avoid Family gatherings."

"What he means is he doesn't want to run into his exes," I throw in. "Especially since half of them were already married when he slept with them."

"Makes sense." Isabella smirks at my brother. "Are you still sleeping with Franco's daughter?"

Damian swirls his wine and stares at her. "How do you know about that?"

Isabella just smiles and reaches for the carafe with juice.

"I'm not sitting at the same table with that woman!" My daughter's high voice reaches me.

I turn around in my chair and fix Rosa with my stare, making sure she sees in my eyes what I think about her yelling. "Come here."

"No. I told you . . ."

"Right this second, piccola."

She stomps her foot on the floor, juts her chin, and marches over to the table, taking a seat on the other side of Damian.

"Now, apologize to Isabella," I say.

"No."

Jesus. Doesn't puberty hit around twelve or so? Rosa is only seven, but I'm starting to believe she's going into it prematurely. When I told her that Simona and I were divorcing, her comment was "Good riddance." The two of them never had any kind of relationship, and Rosa spent more time with our cook than with her own mother. I talked with Rosa last week and explained the situation with Isabella, and she seemed reasonable, but I guess we'll have to discuss it some more. No matter how or why Isabella ended up here, I will not allow anyone to disrespect her, my daughter included. And I certainly won't allow yelling in my house.

"Are you sure?" I ask.

"Yes."

"Okay. You can go back to your room."

"What?" She bulges her eyes at me. "And dinner?"

"No apology, no dinner."

"Dad!"

"You are free to go." I nod toward the door, and motion with my hand to the maid to serve the food.

"Fine," Rosa snaps, jumps up from the chair, and marches away.

I follow Rosa with my eyes as she leaves and notice Isabella watching me, her mouth pressed into a thin line. I wait to see if she'll comment, but she doesn't say anything, just turns away and focuses on her plate. She probably thinks

I'll let my daughter go to sleep without dinner, and I don't plan on reassuring her.

Isabella

I thought finding the kitchen would pose a problem, but when I get down to the ground floor, one of the maids I met when I arrived is dusting the lamp in the corner.

"Anna, can you show me where the kitchen is?" I ask as I approach her.

She blinks at me with a slightly confused expression on her face, then nods quickly. "Of course, Mrs. Rossi. This way."

I follow Anna down the corridor on the right until we reach the rear of the house, where she stops in front of a white door. "It's here."

"Thank you," I say and step inside.

The kitchen is spacious. Counters and an island on the left. On the right, there is a long wooden table that can seat at least ten people. That's probably where the staff eat. I head over to the cabinets, where a willowy woman in her fifties is polishing glasses by the sink.

"Can I help you, Mrs. Rossi?"

"Would you mind making me a sandwich? I'd do it myself, but I have no idea where you store the ingredients."

"Right away." She nods and rushes around, taking out a plate and bread, then asks, "Do you want something specific?"

"It's for Rosa. Just make them how she usually likes them. Thank you."

The maid busies herself preparing the food, but I notice

her throwing looks my way every couple of seconds. When she's done, she brings over a plate with two sandwiches and a napkin, offering these to me.

"Ham. With extra cheese."

"Thank you, Grace. Good night."

Her eyes widen at hearing me say her name, but she quickly composes herself. "Good night, Mrs. Rossi."

I carry the sandwiches to the third floor, walk down the hallway, and knock on Rosa's door.

"I'm not here!" comes from the other side.

I roll my eyes. It's like I'm listening to my sister. Andrea gets extremely cranky when something is not going her way. I grab the knob with my free hand and open the door. Rosa is lying on her stomach across the bed, fully engrossed in whatever's happening on the phone set in front of her.

When she sees me standing in the doorway, she springs up, staring at me. "What are you doing in my room? Get out or . . ." Her eyes land on the plate in my hands. "No mayo?"

"No mayo." I approach the bed, place the plate next to her, and turn to leave.

"How did you meet my dad?"

I stop. "He jumped into the pool and saved my life."

"You're lying."

"Nope," I call over my shoulder. "Ask him yourself if you want."

"He really saved your life?"

I smile inwardly and turn around. "Want to hear about it?"

"Yes!" she exclaims, her eyes wide. "Tell me."

I plop down on the small sofa in the corner of the room and lean back. "I was a little bit younger than you. It was my sixth birthday party. All of us kids were running around the garden playing. One of my shoelaces was untied, and when I kneeled to tie it right next to the pool, my friend's cousin ran by me and pushed me into it."

"You fell into a pool?"

"Yup."

"And Dad saved you?"

"Jumped right in, clothes and all. The pool wasn't deep, but I was little and could have drowned."

"Wow," she says, then tilts her head, regarding me. "Is that why you married him? Because he saved your life?"

I laugh. "No. I married him because my grandfather and your father agreed that it would be for the best. It's how things sometimes work."

"So, you don't love him?"

Do I? To truly love someone, I would need to love the person the way they wholly are, the best and the worst about them. I've been in love with the idea of Luca since I can remember, and I've been obsessing over him for the last few years like a crazy woman. Is that love? Or just a crush? I've never felt anything similar for another man, that's for sure.

"I like him." I nod.

"I heard Tiyana's sister say my dad is hot. What does that mean?"

I blink, slightly confused about how to explain. Rosa is only seven, even if her attitude screams preteen at times. "It means he looks nice."

"Oh. Okay." She takes a bite of her sandwich, her gaze never leaving me. As she chews, she narrows her eyes as if she's judging me. "Will you yell at me?"

"No. Why would I do that?"

"Simona always yells at me." She shrugs. "When Dad's not around that is. He doesn't allow yelling."

She calls her mother by her first name? I'm still trying to process that fact and the implications it carries when the door opens. Luca steps inside, carrying a tray with a sandwich on a plate and a glass of milk. He halts in the doorway, zeroing in on the sandwich in Rosa's hand.

"Isabella beat you to it," Rosa says between bites and points her finger at me.

"Okay, I'll be going now." I stand up and head toward the door. "Good night, Rosa."

Luca doesn't move from the doorway where he's glaring at me like a hawk. I look up and meet his gaze, and our eyes lock in silence for several long heartbeats until he finally steps aside. Making sure my movements are deliberately slow, I tread down the hallway until I reach my room. Something, call it intuition, tells me he's still watching me as I slip inside my room without looking back.

The moment the door closes behind me I exhale and lean my back against it. I thought it would be easy to pretend I'm indifferent, but I have a feeling that a single kind act on my part will result in him pulling away even more. I can't risk it. Not yet.

Being so close to Luca after all these years and knowing he doesn't want anything to do with me . . . hurts. In a way, it was easier when I knew I didn't have a chance. I never expected anything. And now, when I finally have him so close, it feels like he's even farther away than he was before.

I close my eyes and remember the day of my eighteenth birthday when he called me tesoro. Apparently, the word didn't really carry the affection I imagined. It was just a word said in passing. Yet, I thought about that moment and his light touch on my hair for days after it happened.

Well, I'm not giving up. He better prepare for war, because that's what I'm going to serve him. I will fight him and his indifference, every step of the way.

"You better be ready, Luca Rossi," I whisper to the empty room, "because all's fair in love and war."

Chapter five

Luca

I throw my jacket onto one of the recliners in my room and sit down on the edge of the bed, listening to Donato's mumbling coming from the phone. There have been some problems with one of the properties we bought and I spent last night and the whole of today in my office downtown, trying to get that shit sorted out. I really don't need another fuckup today.

"Oh, for the love of God, Donato. Can't you deal with at least some of the shit by yourself?" I say into the phone, squeezing the bridge of my nose. "How many crates?"

"The truck just came in. We opened the first few, but it's likely several more are the same, Luca."

"Fuck." I close my eyes in frustration. What the hell am I going to do with a whole fucking shipment of the wrong caliber ammunition?

A low, moaning sound reaches me from the direction of Isabella's room and I look up, staring at the door connecting our rooms. I haven't seen her after yesterday evening when I found her in Rosa's room. She brought my daughter dinner. I'm not sure what to think about that. Or about the fact that I've been thinking about her the whole day. Fuck. I need to tell Viola to move her things back to the room across from Rosa's.

"What should I tell the Romanians?" Donato asks, pulling me away from thinking about my young wife.

"Call Bogdan. Tell him I'm expecting him at the warehouse at eight tomorrow morning."

"What if he says he can't come?"

"Then, I will come to him and personally put each and every fucking bullet up his ass. Tell him that." I throw the phone onto the bed. Damn Romanians.

I cross my bedroom, heading toward the bathroom, but stop in front of the connecting door to the room where Isabella is sleeping. There it is again, another quiet moan like the one I thought I heard a few moments ago. I inch closer to the door, wondering if something's wrong, but there's only silence from the other side. The door handle feels cool when I grasp it and open the door as quietly as possible, taking a peek inside.

At first, I think Isabella must be unwell, because the only thing I can see through the darkness is her body on the bed, twisted slightly to the side. I open the door a bit more and some of the light from my room spills inside, allowing me to see her more clearly. The moment I do, my hand tightens on the handle.

Isabella lifts her head off the pillow and looks directly at me while her hand keeps moving inside her silky pajama pants, right between her legs. I watch, mesmerized, as she lifts her ass up and a moan escapes her lips. My breaths quicken and I feel myself getting hard as she opens her legs wider and slides her other hand under the waistband. I should turn around and shut the door in my wake, but I can't make myself leave. I'm glued to the sight of my teenage wife as she pleasures herself, her eyes fixed on me the whole time. She lifts her pelvis again and starts panting, her lips partially open. I grip the doorjamb with my other hand when she arches her body and throws back her head as tremors shake her frame. It lasts a few seconds before she sags down onto the bed. She exhales slowly, removes her hands from inside of her pants, and flashes her eyes at me one more time as she slides under the blanket.

I stare at her for some time, then turn around and bang the door closed.

Isabella

"Good morning," I smile at Rosa and Damian as I sit down at the dining table where coffee has already been served.

"You seem to be cheerful today. Any particular reason?" Damian asks and reaches for his coffee.

Of course I am, and there's a very specific reason. Every time I think about the shocked look on my husband's face when he opened the door and saw me playing with my pussy, a smile pulls at my lips. Yes, he went back to his room and banged the door after him, but based on the way he gripped the doorway while he watched, we're off to a good start.

"No reason." I nod toward the empty chair on my left. "Where's Luca?"

"There were some problems he had to deal with, so he left early. He was in a really strange mood, though," Damian says, looking at me over the rim of his cup.

"Oh? How so?"

"Cranky. Snapping at the staff. He rarely does that. I wonder what could have riled him up."

"He's in a stressful line of work." I shrug, a picture of innocence.

"Yeah, it must be that," he says casually, but I see the way he's looking at me with a tiny smile on his lips.

"I'll need a driver," I say. "My grandfather's not feeling well. I want to drop by and check on him."

"Sure. But we'll have to wait for Luca to come back to see who he'll assign as your security detail."

"I won't need a bodyguard today. I'll be going straight to the don's house and back, I don't plan on stopping anywhere else or leaving the car along the way."

"Luca won't like it if you leave the grounds without one, Isabella."

"Dad always has to have the last word, Isa," Rosa throws in, laughing.

Good to know.

A maid brings in a huge basket of freshly baked pastries and places it in the middle of the table. Rosa jumps up, grabbing two croissants, but before placing them on her plate throws a sideways look at me.

"Is something wrong, Rosa?" I ask and reach to take some pastries for myself.

"I'm really hungry," she mumbles.

"Then you should eat those before they get cold." I nod at the croissants she's still holding.

"Both?"

"You said you're hungry."

"But I'll get fat."

My head snaps up. "Oh, sweetie, you won't get fat. Where did you get that idea from?"

Rosa bends her head and shrugs. "Simona told me I need to watch how much I eat because of my meta . . . hm, metalism."

Jesus Christ. Something is seriously wrong with that woman. I place my palms on the table and lean toward Rosa. Damian keeps observing the situation without commenting, as if he's waiting to see what I'll do.

"You mean metabolism, sweetie. You're a child. Kids need to eat a good breakfast because they're still growing." I reach out and, taking the croissants from her hands, lower them onto her plate. "You don't have to worry about your metabolism for at least a decade. Okay?"

A small smile pulls at Rosa's lips, and the next second she digs into her breakfast. When I lean back in my chair, I notice Luca's brother watching me and I raise an eyebrow at him. Damian smirks and gets back to his coffee.

Luca

I walk inside the warehouse where my men are unloading the rest of the crates that came last night. Donato is following a few paces behind me. Bogdan and two more of his guys are standing next to the truck, arguing.

"What happened with my shipment?" I nod toward the crates left on the truck.

"Gavril swapped the model numbers on some containers," Bogdan says and turns to face the tall guy on his right. "I told you to check everything twice!"

"How many crates?" I ask.

"Twelve. I'll have the correct ammunition in two weeks. Three, in the worst-case scenario."

I look back at Donato. "When did we promise to deliver those?"

"On Monday."

I turn back to Bogdan. "I need the correct ammo on Sunday."

"I can't get anything within the next ten days, Luca. All my trucks are already loaded and have routes planned out. How about the weekend after next?"

How unfortunate. I walk to the open crates lined along the truck, take out a Beretta, then reach for a magazine in the adjacent container. "I have a feeling you are not taking our arrangement seriously, Bogdan." I load the magazine inside the gun. "Let's change the narrative."

"Oh, come on. You know how it is. Mistakes happen."

"Indeed." I cock the gun. "The thing is, Bogdan, I've been in an extremely bad mood recently. I didn't need this today."

I lift the gun and shoot the asshole who apparently caused this clusterfuck, hitting his forehead dead-center.

"What the fuck!" Bogdan yells, staring at the dead guy now at his feet.

"You see, I've just mistaken Gavril for you. Mistakes happen," I say and shoot Bogdan's other guy. His body drops next to the first one. "Should I continue? It's only you left. I'm pretty sure I won't make a mistake a third time."

Bogdan's eyes bulge, his mouth opening and closing like a fish out of water.

"I want my ammunition here on Sunday. Can you do that for me?"

He nods.

"Good. I'm glad we've found a language that makes it easier for you to understand." I throw the gun back in the crate. "Ask around and see if you can get me a tank."

My arms supplier just stares at me.

"Can you?" I ask again.

"A tank . . . as in . . . an actual tank?"

"Do you sell imaginary ones as well?" I shake my head. "Belov sounded interested when we met. Says he's asking for a friend."

"They're all insane, those Russians," he mumbles.

"Let me know what you find out."

My phone rings as I'm getting behind the wheel, showing Isabella's name. She probably asked Damian for my number, since I never offered it to her. But I certainly made sure I have hers. It's a shitty move, I know, but I've already been thinking about my wife way more than I should. I don't need her calling me, especially now when all I can think about are the sounds she was making last evening.

I let the phone ring and throw it onto the passenger's seat. Maybe if I avoid her, I might be able to forget how edible she looked last night. The moment I come home I'm ordering her to move out of that damn room.

Isabella

It's already five in the afternoon, and Luca still hasn't returned. I tried calling him several times, but each call went unanswered. Finally, I decide I'm done waiting for him, so I head down to the ground floor and approach the security guy standing at the front door.

"Can you please get me a car and a driver?"

"Of course, Mrs. Rossi. Did Mr. Rossi approve it?"

"I don't need my husband to approve anything for me. Please get me a car."

He fidgets, visibly unsure of what to do, and it looks like I'll have to help him decide.

"Are you disobeying my direct request, Emilio?"

"No, of course not, Mrs. Rossi. I'll get you a car immediately." He quickly takes out his phone.

I don't like pulling rank with the staff, but sometimes it's necessary. Being a woman in mafia circles is not easy. I watched my mother be ignored too many times when she tried to join the "men's conversations" at Family dinners. Even though she has a degree in economics, no one except my grandfather has ever asked for her opinion. The mafia world is ruled by men, and women are often perceived as less important and weak. It is imperative I make my position clear from the beginning if I want to be treated as equal. I've never had a problem with authority in my grandfather's house. Here, on the other hand, even though I'm a capo's wife, they still see a nineteen-year-old girl, and that's not something either Luca or I can afford. He might not have wanted me, but he got me, and I will not end up as a burden or a trophy wife.

I resigned myself to becoming a capo's wife a long time ago. I've been groomed for it since I was ten. While other girls my age were having playdates and obsessing over their latest celebrity crushes, I was learning how to feign interest even when a conversation bored me to death. I learned how to smile and what to say to make people open up and spill information they wouldn't normally share. As well as how to make myself seem a little stupid, if the situation required it. There were key lessons on how to pretend to be having a great time even when the only thing I wanted was to go to my room and be alone. But the most important training I ever received was to never show weakness. Never cry when someone can see, and never show if their words hurt you. In a tank full of sharks, I can't allow myself to bleed, or they would eat me alive.

While my friends stalked cute boys on Facebook and Instagram, I spent hours sitting with my mother at social events, listening to her and learning as she explained who was who in our world and about their roles in the Family. But most of all, I discovered everyone's dirty laundry, and there were lots of it. I smile inwardly at the recollection. How I would love to see the faces of all those men who believed my mother to be just another pretty, harmless face. They had no idea how dangerous she was.

I haven't officially met more than half of the people in the Family, but thanks to my mother, I knew who had affairs with whom, who enjoyed gambling a bit too much, and whose tongue would loosen when they had a few shots. Those may sound like trivial things, but in Cosa Nostra, information means power. And power is the main currency of all the games in the mafia world.

A silver sedan with tinted windows pulls up to the front of the stone steps. The driver gets out, opens the back door and nods at me. "Mrs. Rossi."

"Thank you, Emilio." I smile at the security guard and descend the stairs, heading toward the car. "To the don's house, Renato."

The driver looks at me with surprise, but he tucks his chin and closes the door after me. I quite enjoy the shock on people's faces when I address them by their name. The first lesson my mother taught me was to remember every name of every person I ever meet.

Luca

I knock at the door of Isabella's room, not getting an answer.

She called me several more times today. However, I was still too pissed with myself about last night, so I kept ignoring her. As if not talking to her would somehow erase the image of her arching her back as she masturbated in front of me, or the fact that I had to take a long, cold shower immediately after leaving her room.

I knock again. Nothing.

"Isabella?" I open the door and find her room empty.

I already checked the living room and the library on the ground floor, but she wasn't there. Maybe she's with Rosa. I walk down the hallway and open Rosa's door. My daughter is sprawled on the bed on her back, watching some crap on her phone again.

"Dad?" She looks up at me. "Can I pierce my eyebrow?"

"What? No, you cannot pierce your anything. Are you watching that TikTik again?" I'm going to uninstall that shit from her phone. It's a bad influence.

"It's TikTok, Dad." She giggles. "What about tattoos?"

"You're seven. Forget about tattoos or piercings for the next fifteen years, Rosa."

"When did you get your tats?"

Twenty years ago. But there's no way I'm telling her that. "When I was thirty. You can get yours when you're thirty, as well."

"No!"

I raise my eyebrows at her, "Yes. Have you seen Isabella?"

"She was downstairs for lunch. But I haven't seen her after that." She shrugs and looks back at her phone.

Perfect. Where is that woman? I head down to the second floor where Damian has his rooms. His bedroom is empty, so I go to his office next.

"Where's Isabella?" I ask from the doorway.

"I have no idea," Damian mumbles without taking his eyes off the laptop screen. "The real estate prices went up again. We should sell some of the properties we don't use."

"She's not in her room or anywhere else in the house."

"Then she's probably still at the don's house. I'm selling those apartments we have downtown. They only eat away at the money since you won't allow me to rent them out, and if we—"

"What!"

He looks up at me. "You don't want to sell them?"

"What the fuck is she doing at the don's? Who went with her?" Surely, she wouldn't be so reckless as to leave without a security detail.

"I don't know. I gave her your number and assumed you assigned a bodyguard?"

I close my eyes and curse. She went there without any protection and it's my fault. "I didn't take her calls."

Damian's eyebrows lift. "Why?"

"I've been avoiding her. Who took her to the Agostini mansion?"

"You don't avoid people. Did something happen?"

"Will you answer my fucking question?"

He leans back in his chair and folds his hands behind his head, smiling. "Why are you so concerned all of a sudden? You never cared when Simona went somewhere without informing you."

Because I didn't give a fuck if something happened to Simona. However, the idea of Isabella leaving the house without a bodyguard ignites a surge of panic in my chest.

I take a step inside and pin him with my stare. "Damian."

"Jesus fuck. It was Renato's shift."

I grind my teeth. "Find out who let her leave the grounds without a bodyguard and let them know that if that happens again, there will be consequences. Then, call Renato, and if they're still at the don's, tell him to stay put until I get there."

"Why not send one of the security guys?"

"Do it," I snap and leave the room, hearing Damian laugh the moment I shut the door behind me.

It takes me thirty minutes to get to the Agostini mansion, more than enough time to analyze my erratic behavior and come up with zero conclusions. The chances that something could happen to Isabella between the don's house and mine are almost non-existent, and still, I keep hitting the gas like a maniac. I could've sent Marco to drive over and bring her back. I planned on assigning him as Isabella's bodyguard anyway, but I had this strange compulsion to make sure she was all right.

And the idea of her spending time alone with another man doesn't sit well with me. Maybe I'm feeling overprotective since she's so young. Yeah, that must be it. There's no other explanation.

The guards at the gate let me pass without stopping. When I reach the house, I park next to a silver sedan. I recognize it instantly as one of mine. And that's before I spot the dipshit leaning on the hood.

"Head back home," I bark at Renato the moment I'm out of my car. "And if you ever take my wife off the grounds without a security detail again, you're dead."

"Yes, Mr. Rossi." He straightens, nods, and rushes to get inside the vehicle.

I walk around the mansion to the garden on the far side where I've always seen Isabella while visiting the don and head toward the gazebo. Isabella is sitting in a white iron chair with her back turned to me, and her sister sits opposite her. Andrea sees me first and says something to Isabella, probably warning her about my presence. I expect my young wife to tense or turn around in surprise. Maybe even be a little scared since she knows very well that she shouldn't have left without a bodyguard. Instead, when she turns her head, she looks completely unperturbed.

I grab the arm of the chair and turn it around with Isabella in it, ignoring the screeching sounds the chair legs make against the stone.

"Luca." She blinks at me innocently. "I wasn't expecting you here. Do you want something to drink?"

I grab the other chair arm and bend until we're face to face, staring at her enormous eyes. "Why did you leave the house without letting me know?"

"Oh? Am I obliged to share my daily schedule with you?"

My grip on the chair tightens. Yes, I want her to share her

daily schedule with me. I want to know what she does and where she goes. And that's absolutely idiotic.

"No," I make myself say. "But you can't leave the house without a bodyguard."

"Well, if you returned any of my calls, I would have discussed it with you." She shrugs. "But if it distresses you, I won't do it again."

"Good."

"Does that mean you'll answer when I call from now on?"

Oh, she really likes to push my buttons. It's pissing me off. And it also turns me the hell on. I wonder if she would be just as feisty lying under me, with my cock buried inside her. Just thinking about it makes me instantly hard.

"Maybe," I bite out.

Isabella tilts her head up slightly, and there's a barely noticeable curve to her lips. "Works for me."

"Are you done with your visit?"

"Yup," she says, and the corners of her lips curve a little bit more. "Are we taking the chair with us?"

I let go of the chair and move aside. Isabella gives me a smirk as she walks over to give her sister, who gawked at us in silence through this whole ordeal, a goodbye kiss on a cheek.

"See you on Saturday," Andrea says and cuts a quick glance in my direction.

I follow two steps behind Isabella as she heads across the lawn toward the driveway, trying my best to keep my eyes off her ass. She's wearing white jeans today, paired with a silky navy-blue shirt and high-heeled sandals in the same color. As I leer at my wife, the heel of her left shoe catches on something in the grass, and she stumbles slightly. Instantaneously, I spring forward and grab her around the waist, steadying her. Isabella's body tenses under my hand, but it lasts only for a second or so.

"Thank you," she says, regains her balance and keeps walking, as my hand falls away from her.

I look down at the uneven ground and then at her heels, which are at least four inches high. She'll break her leg in those things. I take two quick steps and wrap one arm around her middle. Placing the other behind her knees, I lift her up. There's a barely audible gasp of surprise, but other than that, she doesn't say a word as her arm settles around my neck. I avoid eye contact and keep my teeth clenched as I carry her, heading to the front of the house.

"Where's Renato?" she asks after I put her down next to my car.

I open the passenger door. "I sent him back."

Isabella arches an eyebrow, then gets inside the vehicle and looks straight ahead through the windshield.

As I reverse, I ask, "What's on Saturday?"

"Our friend is having a birthday party."

"You're going?"

"Yes. Is that a problem?"

"No," I say and squeeze the steering wheel. "You will take two bodyguards."

"Of course."

We drive for some time in silence, but I keep thinking about that party. It will probably be at her friend's house. They'll eat junk food and watch movies. And gossip.

"Where is it?" I ask.

"Where is what?"

"The party. At your friend's house?"

Isabella looks at me and laughs. "We're not twelve. The girls and I are going to a club."

My knuckles turn white from my death grip on the wheel. "Which one?"

"Ural."

"That's the Bratva's club."

"Correct." She smirks.

"You're not going."

"Of course, I am. My grandfather signed the treaty with them, so we're friends with the Russians now. It's perfectly safe," she says. "Milene Scardoni is coming too, and since she's bringing her sister, there's no reason for concern. No one will dare approach us while Bianca's husband is there. You can come as well if you want."

"I'm not going to a teenage birthday party."

"Well, I can't say that I expected you to. You wouldn't fit in anyway."

"How so?"

"You're too old, Luca."

I grind my teeth and focus on the road in front of me, pressing the gas pedal to the floor.

Isabella

I open the top drawer of the dresser and regard my collection of sexy underwear and lacy nightgowns.

Most of them I purchased the same day Nonno told me I was going to marry Luca. I was so damn excited that

I dragged Andrea to the mall to shop for all the lingerie I could find. As I tried on set after set, I imagined Luca tearing each one off my body. When we returned home, I had two huge bags filled to the brim with silk and lace.

Lifting one of the white babydoll nighties, I consider it but change my mind and put it back into the drawer. White won't do. Too innocent. Let's go with the black today. I put on a short black nightgown and matching panties, turn off the lamp and climb into bed. It's showtime.

Just like the previous night, not even a minute after I start, the door connecting my room to Luca's opens, revealing his large form framed in the soft light behind him. He stands at the threshold, his hands gripping the doorframe on either side of him. I can't see his face, only the illuminated shape of his body, but I know he's looking at me.

I let my hand travel even lower and slide one finger inside my pussy, panting. Luca leans forward slightly, but then grips the doorframe even harder as if he's at war with himself about whether to come inside. Is he hard? I widen my legs a bit more and tease my clit with my other hand, imagining his cock inside me instead of my finger. The breath leaving my mouth hitches as my movements become faster, and soon, tremors start rocking my body.

I bite my lower lip and, without taking my eyes off Luca, slide another finger inside. A gasp leaves me as I orgasm, riding the wave for almost a full minute. When I come down from the high, I slowly slide my hand out from my panties, and bring it to my mouth, licking the tips of my fingers. A strange growling sound comes from the direction of the door. I tilt my head to the side, watching Luca's looming figure in the doorway, and spread my legs even more in a silent invitation. He doesn't move from his spot, just stands there stone-still, clutching the frame. Watching me. There's a muffled Italian curse, and then he turns away and goes back inside his room, slamming the door shut after him.

Chapter
six

Luca

I HEAR ISABELLA'S DOOR TO THE HALLWAY OPEN AND barely restrain myself from rushing out to intercept her. I should have prohibited her from going to that club, locked her in her room, and thrown away the key.

There's no reason for me to give a fuck where she goes. She'll have Marco and Nicolas with her, so she will be perfectly safe from harm. And I made sure they know to deter any man who may dare approach her. Still, I keep staring at the laptop without actually seeing the numbers on the screen. I'm too focused on the sound of high heels clicking on the hardwood as Isabella walks by my door.

Five minutes pass. The rumble of a car as it leaves the driveway reaches me through the window. I keep staring at the screen. Seven days. That's how long it has been since she became my wife and she's been fucking with my brain since. It started the first night I caught her pleasuring herself. Until that moment, I had myself convinced she was still a child and that thinking about her in any other way would be sick. Well,

I haven't been able to think of her as an adolescent after that, even though I've tried, because she keeps playing with her pussy every single night. And like the sick fuck I am, I come to watch every time.

I avoid her at all costs during the day, occupying myself with work, but I can't stay away at night. The moment I hear her first moan, I'm drawn to that damn door. And then, I open it and stand on the threshold like some psycho, watching Isabella arching her body with her hand between her legs. The first few nights she wore pajamas, but then she switched to short silky nightgowns, her lacy panties the only thing obstructing my view. They were pink last night, and I barely managed to keep myself from rushing to that bed, tearing the lacy fabric from her body, and using *my* hand on her pussy. Or even better, my mouth.

Two more minutes elapse. I close the laptop. She's seen me watching. And not only that, but she also doesn't stop when she notices me lurking in the doorway. She captures my gaze and holds it like I'm her prisoner, not averting her eyes for even a second until that last moment when the tremors take over her body before she comes. She knows I'm watching every time, and that fact gets me even harder. I've had to find my own release after—in the shower, gripping my cock and imagining I'm inside her until I explode all over my hand. A thirty-five-year-old man pumping his cock in a shower while fantasizing about a nineteen-year-old girl. Jesus fuck.

Just because Isabella acts like someone much older doesn't make it better. Neither does her pretending the next morning that nothing happened. She comes downstairs for breakfast, all regal and composed—impeccable manners and calm face—as if everything is perfectly in order.

Another minute trickles by. There's no way I'm going to that party after her. To a club full of other men. Younger men. I close my eyes and take a deep breath. Fuck.

Jumping up from my desk, I grab my holster and the jacket from the chair, curse again, and leave the room.

There are at least a hundred other women in the club, most of them wearing tight short dresses. And who has the tightest and the shortest one? My wife. And as if that wasn't bad enough, it's white, making her glow like a fucking lighthouse under the neon lights.

I grab a glass of seltzer from the bar, squeezing it in my hand. I don't drink alcohol, but as I watch Isabella from my spot in the dark corner, I'm seriously tempted to start. She's standing at a tall round table, her sister on her right, and Milene Scardoni and two girls I don't recognize on the left. Nicolas and Marco are a few paces behind her, watching the crowd. I notice Bianca Scardoni perched at the end of the bar, clutching her Russian husband around his neck and smiling as he whispers something in her ear. Mikhail Orlov at a nightclub. I shake my head. Now I've seen everything.

There's a group of guys at the table next to Isabella's. I noticed them the moment I came in. One of them in particular. He's in his early twenties, blond, and wearing a tight black T-shirt. He's leaning his elbows on the table in a way that showcases his meager-looking biceps. My grip on the glass in my hand tightens. Milene and the other two girls are looking in his direction and giggling, but he's focused on my wife, or more specifically, her cleavage. Isabella doesn't look at him. She seems to be interested in Bianca Scardoni and her husband. As I watch, the blond kid calls the waiter, says something in his ear, and motions with his hand toward Isabella. The waiter nods and leaves. Did that little shit dare send my wife a drink?

The glass in my hand shatters.

Isabella

I can't take my eyes off Milene's sister and her husband. They've been at the bar since we arrived, and despite the crowd, they seem oblivious to anything happening around them. I don't ever remember seeing a man look at a woman the way Bianca's husband looks at her. It's as if she is the single most important being in the whole universe. I want that. I would kill to have Luca look at me that way, to be his sun and sky and everything in between.

I was at their wedding. Everybody was. It's not often that the Bratva and Cosa Nostra decide to ally themselves in such a way. I still remember the collective gasp when it became clear who Bianca Scardoni was marrying. Everyone assumed it was going to be the blond, cocky guy—Kostya. But, when the huge, dark-haired man with a badly scarred face and an eye patch stepped up in front of the wedding officiant, I was in shock, along with everyone else. Bianca doesn't seem to give a damn about her husband's ruined face or that he's missing an eye, because she's gazing at him like he's the most beautiful man on earth.

A waiter approaches, obstructing my view of the couple, and places a bottle of white wine on the table in front of me.

"Miss," he says, "the gentleman from that table has sent this for you."

I don't get the chance to reject it because a hand reaches over from behind me, grips the bottle, and thrusts it back into the confused waiter's chest.

"*Mrs.* Rossi is not interested," Luca's deep voice barks above my head.

I take a deep breath. He came. I feel this silly need to squeak with happiness, but I bottle it up and school my features, glancing at him over my shoulder. "You were in the neighborhood?"

"Yes," he says, his eyes focused on the table next to ours.

Yeah, right. I sigh and take a sip of my orange juice.

I've been drunk just once in my life, from barely two glasses of wine on the night of my eighteenth birthday. After the guests left, I stole a bottle from the kitchen and dragged Andrea to my room so she could keep me company at my personal pity party. I was lucky there was no one except her to witness it, because from what Andrea told me in the morning, I giggled like a crazy person at first, talked about Luca for two hours, then cried and vomited in the toilet for the rest of the night. The only two things I remember were singing "Total Eclipse of the Heart" by Bonnie Tyler, and Andrea holding my hair while I puked my guts out. I haven't touched alcohol since. Not because I have something against it, but because I don't want to risk blurting out anything Luca-related with someone else around.

As I sip my juice and watch the crowd, I wonder if he's going to do anything, maybe start a conversation or touch me. He doesn't. Instead, he stands right behind me, unmoving and silent, looming like a gargoyle. The guy from the nearby group throws a look in my direction, and the next instant, Luca's arms materialize on either side of me, his hands gripping the edge of the table. I close my eyes for a second, trying to calm my inner turmoil. Surrounded by his body on nearly all sides, inhaling his cologne, and not daring to touch him is making me crazy. What would he do if I turned, placed my hands around his neck, and pulled his head down for a kiss? Dear God, I've been imagining how it would feel to be kissed by Luca for so long, but it's too soon. He needs time to get over his issues with our age differences. I won't risk him pulling away even more. I give myself a couple of seconds more to relax, then open my eyes.

"What happened to your hand?" I ask, looking at a piece of cloth that seems to be a kitchen towel, wrapped around his left palm.

"I cut myself on broken glass," comes the answer from above my head.

Where did he find broken glass, for God's sake? "It's still bleeding. You should head home and get that cut cleaned."

"I'm fine."

He's fine. I roll my eyes.

I turn toward Andrea, who's pretending to be interested in something in front of her, but I know she's listening. "I'm going home. Do you want to stay?"

"Yeah, I'll head back with Milene."

"Marco and Nicolas will stay with your sister," Luca says.

"They can go home. Gino is with her." I nod toward my sister's bodyguard who's leaning on the wall further back, then give Andrea a kiss. "I'll call you tomorrow."

RUINED SECRETS

After saying goodbye to the other girls, I turn and leave, with Luca following right behind me—my silent, towering shadow. We're almost at the exit when the guy who was ogling me earlier and three of his friends cut us off. He says something in Russian and smiles, nodding in my direction. The next moment, all of his buddies lunge at Luca.

I stare, petrified, as one of them swings his fist at Luca's head. Luca ducks and grabs the guy's shoulders, then smashes his knee into the man's stomach. One of the remaining two guys grabs Luca from behind, and the other one punches his fist into Luca's side. A hand wraps around my upper arm, pulling me backward into the gathering crowd.

I scream and try to escape, not taking my eyes off Luca, who's managed to get free and is in the process of making mush out of his attacker's face. The person holding me tugs at my arm again, and I turn to see the guy who sent me the drink. I knee the bastard's balls with all my might. He cries out and doubles over, clutching his crotch.

When I look back to where Luca was earlier, the fight seems to be over. One of the assailants is lying on his side, unconscious. Luca has the other guy pressed face first to the floor, holding the man's arm bent behind his back. I don't see the last asshole immediately because the huge frame of Bianca's husband is obstructing my view. Mikhail has his hand wrapped around the guy's throat, keeping him pressed to the wall. The man's feet dangle a foot off the ground. Luca rises and pushes his guy toward the security staff who drag him toward the exit.

I run toward Luca as he turns to look for me. When I approach, his arm shoots out, grabbing me around my waist and pulling me to his body. He takes my chin with his free hand and tilts my head up.

"Did he hurt you?" he asks in a low voice.

"No," I choke out.

Luca nods and exhales, his nostrils flaring. "You're not wearing that dress ever again."

"Okay." I blink at him. Is he going to kiss me? Our faces are so close, and based on the way he's staring at me, it seems like he might. I stop breathing and wait.

"Let's get your sister and friends," he says and releases my chin. "I don't want to see any of you in a Russian club again."

Looks like I'm not getting that kiss after all. As we walk back toward the table to get Andrea and the girls, I barely manage to bottle up the need to scream in frustration.

Luca doesn't say anything during the thirty-minute drive home, and I pretend I'm engrossed in watching the street through my window. When we arrive at the house, he opens my door for me and follows me inside and then up the two flights of stairs until we reach our bedrooms. Looks like we're back to cold shoulders and silent treatment.

"I'm going to shower and then I'm coming to check your hand." I say casually and go inside my room.

If the situation was different, I would have taken care of his cut before doing anything else, but I need time to decompress from the emotional overload before I can continue acting indifferent. Why is he making this so hard, damn it?

After I'm done with the shower, I dress in one of the short silky nightgowns that reveals my cleavage, and head through the door connecting our rooms. I have no intention of making this easy for him.

I don't see Luca anywhere in his bedroom, but the door to the bathroom is open so I turn that way and stop at the threshold. He's standing at the sink in nothing except loose black sweatpants, and for a moment, I find it hard to draw my next breath. I've never seen Luca shirtless, and I can't take my eyes off the perfection that is his body.

He is more muscled than I could have guessed. Those dress shirts hide way too much. Other than his build, they also hid the ink. There's a black geometric pattern forming a sleeve around his right arm, while on his left shoulder and bicep, there's another black and gray design. The front of his torso is free of ink, but I can see there's something that looks like a huge bird in flight on his upper back. However, what catches my attention the most is his hair. It's wet and hangs loose, reaching his shoulder blades. The only time I've seen his hair unbound was thirteen years ago, and seeing it like this now hits me right in the chest. The moment feels somehow intimate.

He's holding his hand over the sink under the spray of water. I gasp as I see his condition. "Oh God."

There's a deep gash in the middle of his palm, and the blood is still oozing out of it. I can't determine exactly how much because it's quickly being washed away.

Luca looks up at me, his eyes stopping at my nightgown's deep V-neck for a few seconds, then he quickly shifts his gaze and turns off the water.

"It looks worse than it is," he says without giving me another glance.

"That will need stitches."

"Damian will patch me up when he comes home."

He takes a towel, wraps it around his palm, then reaches for the first aid kit next to the sink. Stepping inside the bathroom, I stand beside him, take the first aid kit from his hand, and start taking out compresses and bandages. Choosing the largest pack of dressings, I tear the packaging and fold the gauze several times.

"Remove the towel," I say, willing my stomach to stop churning. It's an understatement to say I'm not very good with blood.

Luca does as I say, and I quickly press the folded gauze to the gash. Keeping it in place with my left hand, I roll the self-sticking bandage around his palm.

"Tighter."

I nod, back up the roll, and pull a little more on the bandage, trying to control my erratic breathing. He's so close that if I lean forward just a little my forehead would be pressed against his chest.

"Tighter, Isabella," Luca says next to my ear.

My fingers start shaking slightly, and I'm sure he notices it but he doesn't say anything. When I'm done, I secure the bandage, take a deep breath, and lift my eyes to find him watching me. His face is set in hard lines, his jaw tight. *Do something, damn it! At least fucking touch me*, I want to yell at him. Instead, I just stare as he turns away and leaves the bathroom.

I want to scream. I have to fight with all my will not to run after him and hit him on his chest as hard as I can. Maybe then he would perceive even the slightest amount of the pain that tears me from the inside out every time he turns his back to me. I want to jump into his arms, bury my hands in his hair, and kiss him frantically. Everywhere. But I do neither of those things, only return to my room.

Will he be waiting for me to start my evening show so he can come to watch again? It's okay to observe, but not to touch? Do I have the fucking plague? Well, fuck him. He can wait all night long.

I leave my room, descend the two flights of stairs, and turn left into the kitchen. It's almost one in the morning and there's no one around, so I start opening the cupboards one by one until I find a stash of wine. I take the first bottle I see, pick up the bottle opener and a glass on my way out, and climb the stairs back up to my room.

I fill the wineglass almost to the brim and leave the bottle on the nightstand. On the bed, I sit with my back against the headboard, glass in one hand, and grab my phone from beside the wine bottle. I have a playlist of rock ballads I listen to when I'm feeling down, so I put it on. Drinking alone and humming along to Bon Jovi. Pathetic. Well, nothing new there.

I'm on my third glass when the door between our rooms opens. Looking up from my phone, I find Luca standing in the doorway, staring daggers at me.

"No show tonight," I say, and close my eyes.

For a few seconds, there's only silence, and then I hear the muffled sound of bare feet padding across the floor in my direction.

"You are too young to drink alcohol, Isabella."

I can't help but laugh. What a hypocrite. I open my eyes. He's standing by my bed, his arms crossed over his chest and lips pressed into a thin line. His hair is tied up again. What a shame.

"So, you're saying I should throw this away?" I raise my eyebrows and nod toward the glass in my hand.

"Yes."

"All right." I shrug. Smile. And then splash the contents of the glass into his face. "Any other requests, husband?"

Luca closes his eyes for a second, but when he opens them, the look he gives me is so full of rage that it would have probably made me pee myself if I wasn't drunk. There's also a vein in the side of his neck, one I've always found incredibly sexy, which is currently pulsing. Oh, he is really mad. Suddenly, his hand juts to grab me behind my neck, and he leans forward so our noses are almost touching. The way he's grinding his teeth makes me fear he'll shatter them if he doesn't stop soon.

"You should have told me that this is what it would take to make you touch me." I tilt my chin up. "If I knew, I would have done this the first night."

He removes his hand from my neck immediately. "You are a teenager," he barks. "I don't plan on touching you in any way."

"If that's the case, I'll have to seek out someone else. Someone who *will* fulfill my needs."

"Try," he whispers. "You won't like what will happen." The way his eyes flare makes me tense, but I don't pull away.

"I might be a nineteen-year-old, Luca, but I know what I want and what I need. I want more than my own hand making me come at night." I lean into his face. "If you're not interested, I'll find someone who is. And you don't have the right to deny me that since you obviously won't do anything about my problem."

Luca stares at me with bulging eyes, his breathing

becoming quicker and his nostrils flaring, then he turns his head to the side. There's a loud bang as he hits the headboard with his fist.

"Fine," he says between clenched teeth and turns toward the door to his room. "Have fun."

He walks toward the door, and I try to keep my tears at bay, at least until he leaves the room. I can't believe he would rather let me fuck someone else. When he reaches the door, he stops, gripping the doorway with both hands. He bends his head and stays in that position for quite some time.

A mumbled curse. Another *BAM* echoes through the room as he hits the frame with his palm. A few more curses, and then he turns around and marches back to me.

He reaches the bed in two long strides and, for a long moment, just stands there at the footboard, staring down at me. I suck in a breath and hold it, waiting. It feels like my heart has stopped beating. Suddenly, he leans forward and wraps his hands around my ankles. With a sudden jerk, he pulls me toward himself. The glass I've been holding slips from my hand and falls onto the thick carpet next to the bed.

There's a tick in Luca's jaw and his brow furrows as he bends and grabs the hem of my nightgown in his fists. His forearms ripple with the flex of corded muscles as he tears my nightie in one swift tug. He's angry. It's obvious in his every move and by the way he's clenching his jaw muscles. I don't care. I've been waiting for this so long, and I'm going to take it any way I can get it and love every moment of it.

My breath hitches when he kneels on the floor and places my legs over his shoulders. He buries his face between my legs, and inhales. I bite my lower lip, feeling my wetness soak through the lacy panties, the only barrier between my pussy and his mouth. But he doesn't remove them. Instead, he presses his lips onto the lace, just over my core, and exhales. I grab onto the bedcover and arch my back, almost coming just from feeling his warm breath. The rough skin of his palms brushes my thighs as he slides his hands up to my waist and slips his fingers into the waistline of my panties. His forearms flex again, and there's another tearing sound. He removes the scrap of fabric that were once my panties and a moment later I feel his tongue.

The first lick is slow. Teasing. I squeeze the bedcover harder as tremors pass through my body. He licks me again, then thrusts his tongue inside my opening for a moment before he starts sucking on my clit. I'm already panting, but as he adds his finger, I feel the pressure building more and more. A second finger enters me, and I close my eyes, whimpering. I rip out his hair tie and thread my hands in his hair. The feel of it between my fingers is more than I ever could have imagined. It's still wet, either from his shower or the wine I threw at him. His tongue circles my clit, then he sucks at it, and at the same time, he does something with his finger inside me. I let out a loud moan as my whole body starts shaking. I feel weightless, like I'm floating on air. When he places his thumb on my clit next to his tongue and applies a little pressure, I explode.

My legs are still quivering when he lowers them off his shoulders, and I have no energy left to move any part of my body. Luca rises, sliding his arms under my back and knees, and shifts me to the center of the bed.

He covers me with a blanket and bends down to whisper in my ear, "If I see any other man touch you, he will die. It will be a very unpleasant death." He adjusts the blanket around my shoulders. "And you won't be satisfying your own pussy anymore. When you need your problem, as you called it, taken care of, you come to me. You got that, tesoro?"

"Yes," I rasp.

He nods and heads back into his room, leaving me sated, and absolutely shocked.

Chapter seven

Isabella

IF I EXPECTED LUCA'S COLD TREATMENT TO CEASE AFTER what happened last night, I would be gravely mistaken. When I make it downstairs for breakfast, he's already there with Rosa and Damian. Rosa throws the last few pieces of food in her mouth and rushes off to her room to pack her things for the day she's spending with her mother. Luca gets up shortly after her, saying he has work to do, and vanishes, leaving Damian and me at the table.

"What's going on between you two?" Damian asks the moment Luca is out of view.

"Nothing." I take a sip of my juice. "Why do you ask?"

He leans back in his chair, crossing his arms, and smiles. One thing I've noticed about Damian is that nothing escapes his attention. He might come across as nonchalant, always smiling and joking around, but his eyes betray him. There is pure intellect and calculation hidden there. He's playing his role of a carefree younger brother quite well. If I wasn't so skilled at pretending myself, I might have missed it.

"You're in love with my brother," he says.

Yes, he's definitely more observant than I thought.

"So what?" I ask and continue eating. There's no point in denying it.

Damian laughs and shakes his head. "Since when?"

"Years." I shrug. "What gave me away?"

"The way you look at him when you think no one is watching. Does he know?"

"Nope. And you won't tell him."

"I wasn't meaning to. Your relationship is not my problem. But why not tell him?"

I debate if I should explain or not. He already knows I'm in love with Luca. Maybe he'll have some insight regarding his brother's idiotic behavior.

"Because he treats me like I have the plague," I say. "He can't get over our age difference. He sees me as a child."

Damian starts stirring his coffee with a spoon even though I saw him doing so not a minute earlier.

"Yes, I see how that could be an issue for him," he finally says and looks up at me. "Luca and I are half brothers. His mother killed herself when Luca was a baby."

I blink. I didn't know that, and I was certain that Damian and Luca had the same parents. How come I've never heard about this? "Okay. How does that reflect on my situation?"

"Luca's mother was eighteen when she married our father. It was an arranged marriage." Damian says. "Father was forty."

I close my eyes. Shit.

"From what I know, Luca's mother wasn't mentally stable," he continues. "Couldn't deal with the obligations that came with the position of being a capo's wife, or being married to someone so much older than her. Our father was a hard man. She was young and sheltered. Eventually, she crumbled under the pressure."

"So, what did your brother expect when he agreed to marry me? That we'd be living like roommates until he deems me old enough to upgrade my status to a wife and have sex with me?"

Damian cringes. "Probably."

"Oh, he's in for a surprise, then."

"Don't push him too much. You've already managed to mess with his head quite well. Luca is hell to deal with when he's agitated."

"I don't think I messed up anything. He still doesn't give a fuck about me."

Damian takes a slow sip of his coffee but doesn't remove his eyes from mine. "Do you know what my brother did when he found Simona in bed with her bodyguard?"

I gulp my juice. "She cheated on him?" Who in their right mind would cheat on Luca?

"Luca shot the bodyguard in the head, and threw Simona out, naked, in the middle of the night. When the maid told me what was happening, I came out of my room to see if he was okay." He shakes his head. "Luca told the staff to clean up, greeted the girl I had over, then climbed up to the third floor, and went to bed. The next morning, he said he hadn't slept that well in ages."

"So?"

"So, imagine my surprise when I saw him storming out of the house last night, furious. I asked what was going on, and he said, and I quote, 'She went to a fucking club,' then got into his car and was gone in seconds." Damian bursts out laughing and gets up from the table. "I never thought I'd live to see a day when my brother chased after a woman."

I follow Damian with my eyes, wondering if he could be right. Luca jealous? Because of me?

Luca

"I'm not buying anything before trying out the product, Bogdan," I say into the phone and flip through the papers on my desk. I've spent the whole morning in my downtown office, going over the cash flow of our real estate business.

"It has a twenty-inch barrel and a rifle-length gas system. A candy, believe me," he says.

"How much?"

"They're a steal at seven hundred dollars apiece," he says, "but I'll take six fifty for each if you get more than five hundred."

"I'll take four hundred for six hundred dollars per piece."

"No way, Luca. I'm selling last year's model for that price."

"All right. I'll check with Dushku, then. Maybe he can work with that price."

"You're not going to the Albanians!" he barks. "We agreed on exclusivity two years ago."

"We also agreed that you will be delivering the goods I ordered," I say.

"It was a one-time fuckup, and you were very clear in showing your displeasure."

"I'm glad to hear that." I turn the page and skim the

numbers on the next one. "I'll take four hundred pieces at six hundred dollars a pop. Or I go to Dushku."

"Fuck you, Luca," he says, then mumbles something in Romanian. "Okay. Anything else?"

"A sample for me to try out first. If I like it, we are a go. Send me ten more crates of grenades, as well. And Bogdan, if I receive the wrong goods again, you're done. Are we clear on that?"

There's more mumbling in Romanian and then, "Very. I'll call you next week to confirm the shipment details." Bogdan bites out and cuts the call.

There's a knock on my office door, and Donato comes inside. "Luca. What's going on?"

"We have a problem, Donato. Have a seat." I nod toward the chair on the other side of the desk and put the stack of papers in front of him. "This is the cash flow statement from the real estate business."

He takes the printout and starts looking over the numbers. "This seems fine."

"On its own it's good, but not when it can't keep up with the revenues from gun sales." I take the sheet of paper with the expected profits I calculated from the weapons deals and place it over the one he's looking at. "We need the real estate figures to double so Damian can launder all the money. Sit down with Adam and find me some properties that require significant investments. Damian says he can clear at least five million a month through renovations expenses."

"Okay." He nods then looks at me sideways.

"What is it?"

He fidgets in his chair like he usually does when he's delivering bad news. Even though both of us hold the same spot in the hierarchy, no one really considers him a serious player. The only reason he's still holding the capo's role is because he and the don are childhood friends. Donato is too old and too passive to do any actual work, so I'm doing most of it and he's just overseeing execution.

"Barbini reached out to me yesterday," he says.

"And what did Lorenzo want?"

"He was asking about your plans for when you take over."

That didn't take him long. I expected Lorenzo to make a move, but I assumed he would wait until Giuseppe stepped down. "Plans for what exactly?" I ask.

"Family business."

"I'll let the Family know when the time comes. For now, we operate as the don wants."

"Oh. Okay. I'll tell him that." He nods and hurries out of the office.

I pick up my phone and start scrolling through the missed calls from this morning, stopping when I reach Isabella's name. She's called me twice, the first time around ten and again two hours ago. I let it ring through both times. Leaning back in the chair, I tilt my head and stare at the ceiling, wondering what I'm going to do with her.

I have no idea what came over me last night, but no way am I doing it again. And I am not having sex with her until she is twenty-one. It may sound ridiculous, but I can't stomach the idea of fucking a nineteen-year-old. She might not look like one in the dark while sprawled out on the bed, with her hand between her legs. But then I see her in the morning light, looking even younger with her eyes still puffy from a lack of sleep, and I feel like a piece of shit. This madness stops now. What she does in her room, is her business. Whatever insanity that possessed me to tell her to come to me when she needs her "problem" handled is gone now. I'm not opening that door between our rooms again. If she wants to fuck, she'll have to wait, or find someone else. I don't give a damn.

The phone on my desk rings.

"Yes?"

"Mr. Rossi," my secretary says from the other side. "Your wife is here."

What the fuck is she doing here? "Send her in," I say through gritted teeth and march to the door. A brief glance outside and I find all my employees have stopped what they were doing to gawk at Isabella. They probably heard Magda announce her.

"Back to work!" I snap at them as I watch Isabella approach, her heels clicking on the marble floor. She's wearing a white sleeveless dress that hugs her chest and flares down from the waist, reaching her knees. Her hair is tied at the top of her head in a long straight ponytail, and oversized sunglasses hide her eyes.

She stops in front of me, removes the shades, and tilts her head up. "Good afternoon, husband."

"Get inside." I step aside, letting her pass, and shut the door. "Where's your bodyguard?"

"You haven't assigned me one yet. I tried calling you, but you didn't return my calls." She sits down on the sofa in the corner of my office and tilts her chin up. "We had a deal. You take my calls. I take your bodyguard."

"Did Renato drive you here?" He is a dead man.

"No. He said he can't take me anywhere without a bodyguard."

"So how the fuck did you get here?"

"Taxi."

"Are you out of your mind?"

She leans back and smiles. "I'm here because of our agreement."

"What agreement?"

"The one from last night," she says, and I stare as she lifts her ass, pulls the skirt of her dress up and removes a beige thong. "I have a problem. And I need you to solve it."

She launches the thong across the room where it falls on my desk.

"I've changed my mind." I round my desk and sit down. Grabbing the lacy undergarment, I sling it back at her. "You're allowed to use your hand. Go home. One of the security guys will drop you off."

She blinks at me, takes the thong, and places it into her purse. "Well, after last night, I decided that my own hand won't do."

I watch as she walks to the door, scrolling through her phone along the way, then puts the phone to her ear. "See you at dinner," she calls over her shoulder.

"Who are you calling?"

"A problem solver," she says and opens the door. "Hey, Angelo. Do you have plans for this afternoon? Perfect, let's meet—" The door closes, shutting out the rest of her conversation.

I glare at the door and start counting to ten to calm myself. One. Let her go. Two. Not your problem. Three. I spring out of my chair, nearly ripping the door off its hinges as I rush out and straight across the open floor space beyond, ignoring the employees who, once again, have ceased whatever they're doing. When I reach Isabella, I wrap my arms around her middle and lift her up. Turning around, I carry her back toward my office. With her back plastered to my chest and her feet dangling several inches above the ground, her ass is pressed right to my cock, which is getting harder by the second.

"Angelo, looks like something came up, I won't make it today." She's still talking on the phone like nothing strange at all is happening. "Yes, I'll call. Promise."

She most certainly won't be calling him ever again. I'll make sure of that. As I enter the office, I shut the door with my foot and let her slide down my body until her heels reach the floor. She starts turning to face me, but I tighten my arms around her, drawing her body to mine.

"Throw away the phone," I whisper in her ear and slide my palms down and over her hips.

I hear her sharp inhale of breath before she lets the phone fall out of her hand.

"The bag and the glasses," I say as I continue moving my hands lower.

Her bag hits the floor, and the sunglasses follow. When my hands reach the hem of her dress, I start moving them back up, pulling the material along her thighs. "Let's see if my hand can do a better job than yours, hmm?"

"I doubt it," she utters and moans as my finger enters her.

I place my right hand at her clit and start massaging in slow, round circles. Meanwhile, I move my left hand towards her center and insert one finger into her wet pussy. The way her gorgeous ass is pressing against me, I'm ready to blow my load. I barely manage to stifle a groan as I fight to regain control.

Shifting my left hand even lower, I remove my finger and

hear her hiss in frustration. I push it back inside, then carefully add another. Jesus, she's tight. Slowly, I curl my fingers and quicken my movements on her clit. Isabella starts to pant and drops her hands, placing them over mine to increase the pressure. I feel her walls spasm around me, so I massage her clit faster, enjoying her mewls as she comes all over my hand a few seconds later.

I bend my head until my lips almost touch her bare shoulder and inhale her scent. She smells like vanilla.

"Can you walk, tesoro?" I whisper.

"Yes."

"Okay. Let's go to the bathroom." I start to pull my finger out, but she keeps her hand over mine, not letting me withdraw.

"Not yet," she says in a raspy voice, pressing harder on my hand, and it almost makes me snap and fuck her on the spot.

"All right."

I wrap my free arm around her middle and lifting her up, carry her toward the bathroom on the left, keeping my finger buried inside her. Her breathing is shallow and hitches a little with every step. We reach the bathroom and come to a stop in front of a small sink. I lift my head, our gazes meeting in the mirror, and I can't decide what I like more—the flustered expression on her face, her huge eyes burning with fire as she regards me, or the sight of my hand over her pussy as my body looms over her.

I reach for the towel and, putting it between her legs, slowly pull out my finger, watching her as she inhales and closes her eyes. After I clean her up, I throw the towel into the sink and grip the edge of the counter on either side of her, lowering my head until my chin rests on her shoulder.

"So, did I resolve your problem?" I ask, holding my eyes fixed on hers in the mirror.

"Yes. Thank you."

"Good. If I catch you calling the little Scardoni boy again, I'm going to break his legs. And his hands. Is that clear?"

The corner of her lips lift upward, but she doesn't reply. Oh, she really likes to defy me.

I move my hand between her legs again and press lightly on her still-sensitive pussy, making her gasp. "Is that clear, Isabella?"

"Yes." She exhales.

"Perfect." I remove my hand and straighten up. "I'll call security. Two of the guys will drive you back home."

I leave the bathroom, sit at my desk, and grab the phone to call security. Isabella walks out two minutes later, her dress straightened and hair no longer in disarray. She bends over to collect her things from the floor, giving me a view of her naked ass, then puts her sunglasses on and heads to the door.

"I like the feel of your hands and mouth on me," she says over her shoulder. "But you know that's not enough. Don't you, Luca?"

She doesn't wait for my reply, just leaves me to stare at the door she vanished through and to wonder how a nineteen-year-old girl managed to so royally fuck up my head.

The ringing of my phone wakes me up. I open my eyes and stare at the ceiling, trying to ignore the ache in my fully erect cock—the result of the dream that haunts me every night. Me, weighing Isabella down with my body, my cock buried inside of her. I thought she'd skip the evening show after what happened in the office this afternoon. She didn't. I tried restraining myself when I heard soft moans coming from her room. And failed miserably. Barely two minutes after the first moan, I stormed inside Isabella's bedroom and feasted on her sweet pussy until she came all over my face.

The ringing stops, then starts again. I grab the phone to see Donato's name on the screen. The numbers in the corner show it's three in the morning.

"What happened?" I ask the moment I take the call.

"I'm at the warehouse. We caught one of the security guards stealing ammunition."

"So?"

"What do you want me to do with him?"

I squeeze my temples between my thumb and middle finger and shake my head. "Kill him, Donato."

"Kill? Are you certain?"

Jesus. How the fuck he ended up being a capo, I'll never understand. I start to tell him to have one of the guys kill the thief then change my mind.

"I'll be there in an hour," I say and cut the call.

I need something to shake loose the frustration.

In the shower, as the water pours down on me, I grip my aching cock and imagine pounding into Isabella from behind, with her ass right there in front of me. It doesn't take any time at all to find my release. Despite jerking off, I'm still wound up as I dress and head outside.

When I reach the warehouse where we store the guns, I head right toward the man sitting in the far corner. Donato is standing next to him, along with another of my guards, both holding guns pointed at him. I'm amazed by the fact that Donato knows how to hold the gun at all.

"Is that the thief?" I ask.

"Yes." Donato nods. "Gianni caught him while—"

I don't wait for him to finish, just draw my gun from the holster, point it at the thief's chest, and fire four times. Donato gasps and stumbles backward, staring at the blood soaking the front of the man's shirt. I turn around and head back to my car, still pissed and sexually frustrated as fuck. Damn that woman. Damn her to hell.

Chapter Eight

Isabella

I REACH FOR THE WATER CARAFE IN THE MIDDLE OF THE table, watching Luca from the corner of my eye. He's been in a sour mood for the last few days, but it hit its peak this morning. He hasn't said a word since he came down for breakfast.

We've been at this status quo for almost three weeks now. We have breakfast with Damian and Rosa, and then he goes to work. Every day at two, I go to his office, where he wrecks me bit by bit with his fingers in the best possible way, and in the evening, he enters my room and devours me with his masterful tongue. He sates me so well the only thing I'm able to do after is fall into a deep sleep.

However, nothing else has changed. He still mostly ignores my presence during the day. He hasn't touched me in any way unless he is "solving my problems," and my patience is slowly running out.

"Is your downtown office just a front or a real business?" I ask as I fill my glass with water.

"It's real," he says without lifting his head, focused intently on the plate of food in front of him. "Real estate business is the best way to launder big amounts of money," he adds after another bite.

"And who's in charge of that?"

"Oh, that would be me," Damian chimes in with a mischievous smile.

I raise my eyebrows. He's barely twenty-three, and we're talking about laundering millions. Luca must have great deal of confidence in his brother's abilities.

"Are you involved in the arms dealing as well, or do you just handle the financial part?" I ask.

Luca's head snaps up. "How do you know about our arms dealing business?"

"Please." I snort. "Where do you think I've lived my whole life? Under a rock?"

"You're the don's granddaughter. You should have spent your days browsing magazines, shopping, and going to spas."

"I'm sorry to disappoint. Spas were never my thing." I shrug. "And because I am the don's granddaughter, I've been groomed for my role since I was ten."

"And what role would that be?"

"The wife of a capo," I say and take a croissant from the basket.

"Who should do nothing but go shopping and to spas and browse magazines."

"Well, I didn't expect to be married off to a chauvinistic grump, but it is what it is."

Across the table from me, Damian chokes on his coffee when he bursts out laughing. "Sorry I just . . ." He snickers. "Chauvinistic grump." He laughs again.

I turn my head and find Luca watching me through narrowed eyes. "I want you to stay in your room this afternoon," he says.

"Why?"

"Simona is coming to take Rosa, and I have a meeting I need to attend. I don't want you two confronting one another, especially when I'm not here."

I reach for the milk and fill the glass for Rosa. When I went to see her earlier, she said she's not feeling well and decided to stay in her room. "You're afraid I'll bite your ex or something?"

"I'm not concerned about what *you* may do, Isabella."

Oh. He's concerned about what his big, bad ex will do to his delicate young wife. How sweet of him. I wish I were drunk again so I could allow myself to throw something else in his face.

"I'll take Rosa her breakfast, then make sure I'm locked away safe in my room when your ex-wife comes." I grab the plate I've prepared for Rosa, turn on my heel, and march toward the stairway.

Damian's laughter rings out behind me.

"Do you want me to get you tea or something?" I ask Rosa.

"No," she mumbles into her pillow.

"Maybe we should call a doctor." I put my palm on her forehead, but it doesn't feel like she has a fever. "Did you eat something strange yesterday?"

"No."

"Diarrhea? Do you feel like vomiting?"

"No, just my stomach hurts. I'm okay."

I sit on the edge of her bed and lightly squeeze her shoulder. "So, this has nothing to do with the fact your mom is coming?"

"She wants me to call her Simona," she says. "And I don't want to go with her. She always takes me to a mall. It's boring."

"Well, can you ask her to take you to the park? Or to see some movie? How about that?"

"She hates parks because I get dirty. And she says she doesn't like movies because her eyes hurt. I want to stay here."

"You'll be bored here, too."

"I won't. I can call Clara. She said she'll bring Tomas next time she comes."

"Who's Tomas?"

"Her cat. He has a little leash so we can walk him around the garden. And Grace will make us sandwiches."

"Did you tell your dad that you don't want to go with Simona?"

"No. He wouldn't understand."

"Of course, he would. Want me to call him to come upstairs?"

"Yeah."

I nod, grab my phone, and call Luca.

"What?" he barks.

A picture of politeness. "Please come upstairs. Rosa wants to talk to you."

"I'm just getting into my car."

"Well *un*-get and come talk with your daughter. It's important."

I cut the call and rub Rosa's back. "He's coming. If you

don't feel like doing something, you should always tell your dad. Okay?"

"Okay."

"I'll be in my room. Come get me if you need me. If you want, we can watch something downstairs later. Or we can call your friend. Deal?"

"Okay."

I squeeze her shoulder again and leave her room.

Luca

"She's your mother, piccola." I brush the back of my palm down Rosa's cheek. "You should spend some time with her."

"I don't want to," she bites out, staring me down. She's trying very hard to keep her tears at bay, but I see how her nose scrunches a little, and a stray tear slides down her cheek. "Please don't make me go with her."

"I will never make you do anything you don't want to, Rosa," I say and gather her in my arms. Rosa sniffs, then wraps her arms around my neck, burying her face in the crook of it. She's always loved doing that, even when she was a baby.

"Promise?" she whispers.

I take her chin between my thumb and fingers and tilt her head up to look into her eyes. "I promise."

"Simona told me she would write to some kind of service that will take me away and make me live with her. I don't want to live with her, Dad."

I squeeze my hand into a fist. "She told you that, huh?"

"Yes."

"That's not true, Rosa. No one can take you away from me. She's just trying to manipulate you."

"Why does she want me to go anywhere with her? She doesn't love me. Why can't she just . . . go away?"

Sometimes I wish I could just kill Simona and be done with it, but I can't do that to Rosa. Simona is still her mother. I press my daughter's face to my chest and wrap my arm around her back. "She loves you in her own way, Rosa. She just doesn't know how to show it."

I'm not sure Simona is capable of loving anyone except herself. Sometimes I wonder if I should have just taken Rosa without marrying my ex, but I didn't want my child to grow up without a mother like I did. I thought Simona would change, so I stayed with her for Rosa's sake. She didn't.

"Can I call Clara to come over?" Rosa asks into my chest. "We can ask Grace to make us tuna sandwiches. And those ginger cookies with cinnamon."

"Only if you leave some for me. You and Clara ate everything the last time."

"Uncle Damian ate them! We told him to leave you some, but he said his sugar level was low and he needed them more than you."

I laugh. Why am I not surprised?

"Isa said she'd watch a movie with me," Rosa adds and leans back to look at my eyes. "I really like Isa, Dad."

"You do?" I brush my thumb over her cheek, removing her tears.

"Yeah. I was working on some math problems we needed to finish during vacation yesterday and asked her to help me. She worked with me the whole morning. Isa is super smart."

"Yes, she is." I nod.

It's the truth. My young wife is one exceptionally intelligent woman. I can't help but admire the way she plays me, day after day, without backing down or faltering her stance. And with every passing day, it's becoming harder to continue resisting. Sometimes, I find myself watching her, debating whether I should just say, "to hell with it," grab her and crush my mouth to hers. I don't remember a time I've been so crazy about a woman before. It's like she's slipped under my skin and made her home there, and it's getting exponentially worse with every day that passes. Every stubborn look, every clever remark, every defiant tilt of her chin—it all contributes to her working her way even deeper into me.

I quickly shake my head and place a kiss at Rosa's head. "I have to go to work but call me if you need me, and I'll come right back. Okay, piccola?"

"Yeah." she nods.

When I leave Rosa's room, I find Isabella downstairs talking with one of the maids. She spots me coming, and her eyes instantly flick away before I can pin her with my gaze. As if my presence makes no difference to her one way or another, she continues her conversation without missing a beat.

"I'll call Simona to reschedule her visit," I say in passing.

"How nice. Does that mean it's safe for me to roam the house this afternoon?"

I decide to ignore her snarky remark and head toward the front door. I'm not sure if Isabella would be able to stand up to Simona, especially if my ex is in one of her moods, and I won't risk them meeting unless I'm there. Simona is a bitch and just the idea of her saying something that might hurt Isabella makes the rage boil in my stomach.

Isabella

I close the book on world economy, one of the courses on my curriculum next semester, and put it into the desk drawer. Since I have nothing to do around here, I've decided to use the time to go over the main subjects and get myself prepared for when classes resume. I doubt my husband knows I'm attending college as an online student, and since he's never actually asked what I do during the day, I've never offered the information.

My phone rings as I'm heading to the bathroom to shower and change before going over to Luca's office. The display shows the number from the gate guard. Strange. I don't remember inviting anyone over.

"Mrs. Rossi," he says when I take the call. "I have Ms. Albano here. She's insisting on being let inside."

What the hell is Luca's ex doing here? He said they'd rescheduled her visit.

"Did you call Luca?" I ask.

"Twice. He's not answering."

Typical. "Let her in, Tony," I say, leave my room, and head downstairs.

As I pass the big mirror at the landing on the second floor, I glance at my reflection and groan. If I'd known Simona would be coming, I'd have put on something else, maybe jeans and a white blouse. And heels. As it is, I'll be meeting my husband's first wife in pastel blue sweatpants and a matching T-shirt, with Hello Kitty face plastered all over my chest. Barefoot. How nice.

I'm halfway to the front door when I hear high-pitched yelling on the other side. The front door opens, and a tall blonde woman rushes inside, her heels clicking on the floor. Our security guard runs in after her.

"I told her to wait outside, Mrs. Rossi," he says. "She wouldn't listen."

"It's all right, Emilio." I nod and return my gaze to Simona Albano, *formerly* Rossi.

I have seen her numerous times at different social gatherings. It was impossible to miss her. Each time, I felt this piercing pain in the middle of my stomach. I envied her so much. The last time I saw her was six months ago, and since then, her lips have doubled in size, her boobs are bigger, and she's lost at least ten pounds. She looks like a clothes hanger for her expensive, beige-with-black-polka-dots dress.

Standing with her hand on her hip, she looks me up and down, pausing for a few seconds on the Hello Kitty image on my chest, and bursts out laughing.

"Dear God, I knew you were young, but I had no idea they made Luca marry a child." She gives me a condescending smile.

"What do you want, Simona?"

"It's Ms. Albano to you."

"You came into my house uninvited," I say. "I'm going to call you whatever the fuck I want."

Simona blinks, looking a bit dumbfounded. She tries to sneer at me in the process, but all she ends up doing is cracking her Botox-infused lips. "I came to pick up Rosa."

"Rosa doesn't want to go. Luca told me he called you and rescheduled it."

"I changed my mind. Where's my daughter? I'm taking her shopping."

"Did you clear it with Luca?"

"I don't have to clear anything with him," she snaps.

"Of course, you do. You signed all parental rights over to him. Rosa is not leaving unless her father says so."

Anger flashes in Simona's eyes. She takes two steps forward until she's standing right in front of me, and her lips stretch into a sneer that transforms her face from beautiful into something grotesque. "Get me my daughter! Right now!"

"Have a nice day, Simona." I turn to Emilio, who's standing in the doorway. "Please walk her to her car and make sure she leaves the grounds. And make it clear to Tony that she is not allowed through the gate again unless Luca has cleared it."

I turn to leave when I feel a hand grabbing my upper arm. "How dare you throw me out? This was my house!"

"*Was*. Past tense." I look down at her hand, then back into her eyes. "Get your hand off me."

"Who do you think you are, you little bitch?" she snaps and starts shaking me.

I'm not a violent person. I believe in resolving problems with discussion, but I won't allow anyone to manhandle me. Especially my husband's ex-wife. I look down, focus my gaze on her toes peeking out from her strappy sandals, then smash my right heel onto them with all my might. Simona screams and lets go of my arm. I use the opportunity to grab a handful of her hair, pulling her head back. She screams again and tries scratching my face, but I move to stand behind her and pull her hair down even further, making her arch her back.

"Don't you dare touch me again!" I bark and drag her toward the door where Emilio is standing, his mouth gaping. "Get her out." I let go of Simona's hair, turn on my heel, and head to the kitchen. I need some sugar because I'm coming down from an adrenaline high and my legs are starting to shake. As I pass the stairway, I hear chuckling and lift my head. Damian is standing next to the banister with his phone in front of him.

"Don't even think about posting that anywhere. I mean it, Damian."

"It's for my private collection of catfight videos." He grins and disappears down the hallway.

Luca

My phone rings with Damian's name flashing on the screen. I let it ring where it's lying on my desk and continue reading the real estate listing I was checking out. He was right. Selling those apartments was a good call. If we had waited, we'd have lost 10 percent. He's probably calling to say "I told you so." I'm not in the mood. It's almost half past two, and Isabella still hasn't come. What if she decided to call the Scardoni pup after all? The ringing stops, only to start again a few seconds later.

I curse and grab the phone. "I'm busy, Damian."

"Simona was here."

"What? When?"

"She just left."

"We agreed to postpone her visit until next week." I hit the table with my palm. "And she knows she shouldn't come into my house unless I'm there."

"Yeah, well, you know Simona."

"What happened? Did she take Rosa?"

"Nope. Isabella didn't let her. She told Simona she can't take Rosa anywhere without your permission."

"Jesus fuck. They met?"

"Yeah. It wasn't pretty."

I stand up from the chair, gripping the phone. "What did Simona do to her?"

"Calm down. Everything's okay."

"Don't tell me to calm down." I take my wallet and car keys from the table and rush out of the office. "I'm on my way."

"Isa is fine. She's watching *Say Yes to the Dress* with Rosa."

"Don't lie to me, Damian. Simona knew I wasn't there, and she came with a purpose. I know my ex all too well."

"I recorded the whole ordeal. I'm sending you a video."

"You recorded it? Why the fuck didn't you throw out that bitch instead?"

"It seemed Isa didn't need my help." He laughs. "She threw her out herself."

"What?" I hit the button on my remote as I approach my car. The doors click just as I'm reaching for the handle.

"Just watch, Luca." Damian cuts the call.

I get into my car and play the video Damian sent. When I come to the part where Simona grabs Isabella's arm, I grip the steering wheel, then reach down and start the car, only to turn it off two seconds later. I watch with growing amazement as my tiny wife grabs my ex, who's more than a head taller, and pulls Simona toward the front door by her hair. The video ends with her casually walking across the hall.

I play the video again, and then one more time. Smiling, I lean back in the seat and shake my head. Little hellion. I step out of the car, intending to call Simona to let her know what I think of her visit, when my phone rings again. The display shows Francesco's name. I don't get calls from Isabella's father often.

"Francesco? What's going on?"

"The don has just been admitted to the hospital," he says. "Another heart attack."

"Fuck. Is it bad?"

"Yes. Can you get Isa there? I haven't told her yet. I was afraid she'd come by herself."

"Sure."

Once he gives me the address, I jump behind the wheel and floor it.

I find Isabella just as Damian said—watching TV with Rosa in the library. Her left arm is lying on the back of the sofa, and as I approach, I notice a red bruise above her elbow. I'm going to kill Simona if she dares come within a five-yard radius of my wife ever again. Without thinking, I reach out and brush her skin with the back of my hand.

Isabella's head snaps up, surprise in her eyes, and I quickly remove my hand.

"Go get your purse," I say and drop a kiss on the top of Rosa's head. "I'll wait for you in the car. We have to go."

"Where?"

"To the hospital. Your grandfather's had another heart attack."

She stares at me for a second, then jumps up from the sofa and leaves the library at a run. I expect her to change or put on some makeup, but she rushes back down the stairs with her purse and shoes on before I reach the front door.

"How is he?" Isabella asks as we get in the car.

"I don't know. Your father just gave me the address and hung up. We'll ask when we get there."

She nods and leans back in the seat, clutching her purse in her lap.

It takes us thirty minutes to reach the hospital and five more to find a parking spot. As soon as I park the car, Isabella gets out and rushes toward the entrance. I run after her, and when I reach her, I take her hand in mine. "Stay close to me."

Isabella looks down at our joined hands, nods, and lets me lead her inside. As we enter the lobby, I scan the people in the waiting room. When I don't notice anything suspicious, I guide us to the information desk and ask for directions.

The closer we get to the hospital unit the nurse indicated, the stronger Isabella's grip on my hand gets. We round the corner and spot two men in front of the door at the end of the hallway and Isabella's father sitting on a chair across from them. Immediately, Isabella lets go of my hand and runs to him.

She embraces her father while he speaks in her ear, probably updating her on her grandfather's condition, and I expect her to break down and start crying at any moment. Instead, she nods, sits down in the chair next to Francesco, and stares at the door in front of her. It amazes me how collected she seems on the outside, because I know she's freaking out on the inside. She couldn't hide the fear in her eyes while we were driving to the hospital. My place is there, sitting next to her and holding her hand, but it doesn't feel right. I'm sure she wouldn't welcome it. Not after the cold shoulder I've been giving her. I've truly been acting like a piece of shit.

Isabella seems to act with more maturity than Simona, who's ten years older. When Damian told me the two of them met today, I assumed I'd find Isabella crying in her room when I came home. I never would have imagined that she'd stand her ground. Damian's video proved me wrong and showed that she managed quite well. My young wife has turned out to be quite a surprise, and I'm finding it hard to continue keeping her at arm's length.

The fact is, I'm attracted to her, and I don't mean just physically. I like the way she stands up to me each and every time—never pulling away and meeting me on the middle ground instead. The way, day after day, she keeps playing the game of indifference that I started, makes me even crazier for her. Maybe I should just let go of my self-restraint and start fucking her senseless. It's not like she doesn't have the experience. That's obvious from the way she's acting. And that realization makes me furious. Why do I care if she's had sex before? And what the hell am I going to do with this idiotic urge to find every man who's touched her and strangle them? Maybe it's her unpredictable behavior that's messing with my brain. She riles me up to the point of my dick exploding one moment, and the next, she's an ice queen, ready to brush me aside for the next schmuck who'll fix her "little problem".

The door to the don's room opens, and Isabella's mother and sister walk out. They exchange a few words, then Isabella heads inside, but not before throwing a quick look in my direction.

Isabella

Dear God, he looks so old.

It's the first thing that flashes through my mind as I enter the room and see my grandfather's fragile form on the bed. I can't reconcile this image of him with how I remember him from my childhood—a burly, tall man, with a deep voice and commanding presence. He always seemed so strong, until his heart started failing him.

"Isi, come here, stella mia," he says.

I sit in the chair next to the bed and take his hand in mine. It feels so light and breakable. I want to say something, but I can't seem to find the words.

"Have I ever told you how much you remind me of your grandmother?" He smiles weakly. "The same big eyes. The same unbreakable spirit that seems so grand for such a tiny person."

He sounds like he is saying goodbye, and I find it hard to rein in the tears. So, I let them fall.

"Don't cry, Isi. I had a good life, and it's time to move on. You have to be strong now, stella mia, because when I'm gone, all hell will break loose. Luca will need you. Especially with the mess Bruno Scardoni has created."

I shake my head and sigh. "I don't think Luca needs anyone, Nonno. He manages quite well on his own."

"Men can be stubborn sometimes. And your husband is the most stubborn one I've ever come across." He raises his hand and brushes my cheek. "I have a confession to make, Isi. I hope you won't get mad that I didn't tell you sooner."

"I can never get mad at you, Nonno. You know that."

He regards me with his dark, slightly misty eyes, then smiles. "I knew, Isi," he says. "I knew for years."

"Knew what?"

"That you were in love with Luca. Still are, from what I can see."

I open my mouth to say something, but he places his finger over my lips. "I paid that bodyguard. The one Luca caught in bed with Simona. It's not like she wasn't cheating on him before, but she was careful not to be caught."

"Nonno!"

"Luca is a good man. And I wanted him for you." He smiles. "So, I made sure you got him, stella mia."

I burst out crying.

"Barbini is going to confront him, Isi. Lorenzo didn't say anything in front of me, but I saw it in his face. Tell Luca to be careful."

"I will," I say through the tears. "But you will be okay,

Nonno. Dad said they're taking you to surgery and the doctors will fix your heart. You're not going anywhere, yet."

"I love you, stella mia."

The door behind me opens and two nurses come in. I squeeze my grandfather's hand and kiss his cheek.

"I love you, too," I say and brush away my tears. "We'll be waiting outside when you come out of surgery. Okay?"

"Okay."

I leave the room and sit next to Andrea, who's whimpering on my mother's shoulder. My father is standing a few paces from us, quietly talking with the doctor. As I turn my head to the right, I see Luca standing at the far end of the long hallway, leaning on the wall with his shoulder. I should go and talk to him, but I don't think I can manage that distance on my shaking legs. Taking the phone from my bag, I press his number and watch as he takes the call.

"The surgery will last several hours. You don't have to stay," I say. "I know you have work to do."

"I'm staying, Isabella."

He puts away the phone and holds his position, looking back at me. Sighing, I lean my head against the wall and close my eyes.

Luca

I hear hurried steps from the direction of the elevator and lift my head to see Lorenzo and Orlando Lombardi approaching. They couldn't have waited until the don was out of the hospital? Bastards. I push away from the wall and head in their direction.

"What do you want?" I stop before them, barring their way.

"We came to see the don," Lorenzo says.

"Giuseppe is in surgery. When we have news, I'll call you."

"Who the fuck do you think you are?" Lorenzo barks into my face. "You can't forbid us from seeing him." He steps forward as if I'll let him pass.

I wrap my hand around his upper arm, stopping him, and get in his face.

"This is a personal matter, Lorenzo. I won't let you or anyone else intrude on Giuseppe's family in this moment. Leave."

"Channeling a don already, Luca?" he spits out. "You couldn't wait to jump into the role, could you? Let go of me!"

"Jesus, Lorenzo." I shake my head and turn to Orlando. "Get him out of the hospital or I will. And I really don't want to make a scene."

"Luca?" Isabella's voice reaches me from behind. "What's going on?"

"Out. Both of you," I say through gritted teeth and release Lorenzo's arm. "Right fucking now."

I watch until Lorenzo and Orlando disappear into the elevator, then turn to Isabella, who's standing a few paces behind me, her arms wrapped tightly around her waist.

"I heard yelling. Is something wrong?" she asks.

"No. They just dropped by to see how Giuseppe is doing. Don't worry."

She nods but doesn't move. She looks so small and so young. I close the distance between us and wrap my arms around her, pressing her to my body.

"He's going to be okay, tesoro," I say into her hair.

"I'm scared," she whispers into my chest.

"I know."

"Mom is freaking out. I better go back," she says but doesn't let me go.

I squeeze her a little tighter. "I'll stay here to make sure no one comes to disturb you. Okay?"

Isabella nods and pulls back, looking up at me. Her eyes are red, but there are no tears. I don't know how someone so young can have such self-control. I'm certain she's keeping her tears at bay with sheer will.

"Thank you," she whispers and walks back to her family.

The doctor comes out at around eleven in the evening, and Isabella's family gathers around him. Based on the looks on their faces, the chances are not good, but the don is still alive. They return to their chairs, and sometime later, Andrea and Isabella's parents stand up and start walking down the hallway toward me.

"How is he?" I ask Francesco.

"In the ICU. It doesn't look good. If he lives through the next twenty-four hours, there's a chance he'll pull through." He puts his arm around his wife's back. "We're going to grab something to eat. Can you stay with Isa?"

"Sure. Bring something for her, as well."

"She said she can't eat."

"Just bring it. I'll make sure she eats it."

When they leave, I walk down the hallway to where Isabella is sitting and crouch in front of her. For a second, I think she must have fallen asleep in the chair, but then she opens her eyes and looks at me.

"How are you holding up?" I ask.

She doesn't answer, just shrugs and closes her eyes again. I can't bear seeing her like this. Beat. Lethargic. With an empty look in her eyes. Reaching out, I cup her cheek with my palm, and her eyes snap open. There it is. That spark I was looking for. I caress her skin with my thumb, noticing how perfectly soft it is. Slowly, she lifts her hand and, after a few seconds of hesitation, cups my cheek just as I have with her. She sighs and leans forward, pressing her forehead to mine.

"What am I going to do with you, Luca?" she whispers.

The sound of approaching steps reaches me from somewhere off to the side, and I assume it's her parents and Andrea returning, but when I rise, I find the doctor from earlier standing a few feet away.

"Mrs. Rossi," The doctor says, an expression of regret all over his face.

"No." Isabella stands up next to me.

"His heart wasn't in a stable condition," the doctor continues. "It stopped while he was waking up from the anesthesia. We couldn't bring him back."

"No." Isabella grabs my hand and squeezes. "Please, no."

"I'm so sorry, Mrs. Rossi. Your grandfather has passed away."

Isabella stumbles. I catch her around the waist and turn her toward me, burying my hand in her hair and pressing her face to my chest. Her parents and sister round the corner and rush toward us. The doctor meets them halfway and gives them the news. Isabella's mother presses her hand to her mouth, and bursts out crying. I look down at Isabella, who is clutching my shirt in her small hands, her silent tears hitting me right in the chest like a sledgehammer. There's nothing I can do to take away her pain, so I just hold her even tighter.

Chapter
nine

Luca

THE RAIN STARTS AS WE'RE LEAVING THE CEMETERY. More than two hundred people attended the funeral, and as the drizzle transforms into a downpour, they run toward their cars for cover. Isabella doesn't change her tempo, and instead stays walking by my side, her head bent. I take off my suit jacket and place it over her shoulders. Her steps falter for a moment and she stops, looking up at me. I can't see her eyes because she's wearing a pair of oversized sunglasses, but I'm pretty sure her cheeks are not wet as a result of the rain. Looks like she's finally allowed herself to cry, but only when there's no one else around.

I open the car door and watch as Isabella gets into the back seat in silence. When she's inside, she moves to the other end and leans her head against the window. She hasn't said a word since this morning. I get inside the car, lean over and wrap my arm around her waist, then pull her onto my lap. A surprised yelp leaves her lips, but she doesn't protest, just places her cheek onto my chest and snuggles into my body.

Her ponytail has loosened, so I remove her hair tie and bury my fingers into her soft hair, massaging her scalp.

When the car stops in front of the house I get out, holding Isabella in my arms as I carry her inside and up the stairs to her room. I put her down next to the bed, expecting her to change, but she just removes my jacket and her sunglasses and slides under the covers. I hate this feeling of helplessness, the inability to make the situation easier for her even just a little bit. So, I do the only thing I can—I carefully remove her heels, arrange the covers around her shoulders and then climb up into the bed behind her. Wrapping my arm around her bundled form, I pull her into my body and stay that way until I hear her breathing even out and she finally falls asleep.

As I stare out the window and look at the setting sun, a realization forms inside my head. Am I falling in love with my wife?

She's nineteen! My brain yells.

I quickly unwrap my arm from Isabella's waist, get up and leave the room, urging myself to forget about that ridiculous idea.

Isabella

I don't remember much of the past two days. What I do remember is Luca carrying me to the car as we left the hospital and me trying without any success to make him put me down. That first night he slept on the sofa which is under the window in my room. The day of the funeral is a complete blur in my mind. I remember the rain and some random moments like Luca holding me inside the car and getting inside the bed fully clothed, but not much else. I'm pretty sure he slept on the sofa last night as well but it looks like he left while I was still asleep.

The sound of a lawn mower invades my thoughts through the open window, and it feels like its rumbling is drilling into my brain. I should get up and close the window but I can't make myself move. Instead, I stay lying on my bed, staring up at the ceiling. My nonno is gone. I can't grasp that fact. This morning when I woke up, I reached for my phone, wanting to call and ask how he's feeling. Like I've done every morning. Only this time my hand stilled halfway to the phone when I remembered.

There's no one around, so I let myself break down and spend the following hour crying my eyes out.

Nonno would be so mad if he saw me now with my puffy face and red eyes. He always insisted on facing whatever life throws at you with your head held high and steel in the spine. I look up at the big clock on the wall. It's seven p.m., and I haven't yet told Luca about my grandfather's warning regarding Lorenzo.

I get out of bed and head into the bathroom to splash some water on my face. Hopefully, it will make me feel a little better. Five minutes later, I leave my room and go to the second floor, hoping to catch Damian in his office.

"Isa?" Damian looks up from his laptop. "Are you okay?"

"I'm fine, thank you. When's Luca coming back? I need to speak with him."

"No idea. He has a meeting with the capos on Friday, so he's trying to tie up loose ends."

"They're swearing fealties to him in four days? That's fast."

"Lorenzo was starting to make trouble," he says. "We had to hurry."

"That's what I wanted to talk with Luca about. Grandfather told me to warn him. Who else?"

"What do you mean?"

I walk up to Damian's desk and take a seat across from him. "Who else is against having Luca as a don? And who's undecided?"

Damian watches me with interest, takes a pen from the table and starts rolling it between his fingers. "Don't take this the wrong way, but why do you ask?"

I smile. "Humor me."

"Orlando Lombardi is against. He sided with Lorenzo and insisted on the Family dropping the arms and gambling deals, and transferring all the efforts into drugs. Luca said no."

"The Bratva has most of the drug business," I say. "It wouldn't be wise butting in, especially after Bruno Scardoni almost killed Bianca's husband." Damian's eyes widen in surprise. Yeah, he wouldn't be the first to underestimate me. "You need to call Orlando Lombardi. Tell him it would be extremely unfortunate if Lorenzo found out what he's been doing every second Saturday morning."

"And what would that be?"

"Banging Lorenzo's wife while she is, supposedly, at her regular manicure appointment," I say. "Who else?"

Damian crosses his arms over his chest and leans back, smiling. "Santino D'Angelo is undecided."

"Well, Santino is not fucking anyone except his maid, and his wife knows about it. Shame," I say. "But his oldest son, Dario, is neck deep in debt. With the Albanians."

"Gambling?"

"Yes. The last bit of information I have is that it's close to three hundred grand, but that was last month. It's probably more now. Dario has a huge influence on his father."

"If we buy out his debt, perhaps he'll be able to steer Santino in the right direction?"

"Most probably." I nod. "Any other problems?"

"None for now." He leans forward, resting his elbows on his desk. "Where did you get this information?"

"Definitely not in spas or from fashion magazines." I smirk. "Don's position is not only about doing the job well. It requires closely watching those who want to stab you in the back, and involves a good deal of blackmailing in order to steer people in the desired direction. My grandfather had Orlando Lombardi's driver on his payroll, as well as two of the maids working for Santino D'Angelo. He had at least one person in each capo's household, and paid them triple their salary to update him on anything that might be useful."

Damian's body stiffens at my words. "He had someone here, as well?"

"Your previous gardener."

"Domenico? The ancient guy who spent half of his time trying to get under Grace's skirt?"

"Well, I don't know whose skirt he was trying to get under while he was here, but he was providing some rather nice intel. He's working for Franco Conti now."

"I'll be damned." He shakes his head. "Giuseppe had his own little nest of spies."

"Yes. My mother and I have been handling them for the last two years since my grandfather got sick. We can continue doing so, but Luca will have to take over the funding."

"I'll talk with him."

"He also needs to call all the big shots in the Family over, after he officially takes over the don position. A month or two from now would work fine."

"My brother is not a fan of parties."

"He'll have to throw one anyway. It's expected."

"You can give Luca a shitload of weapons of any kind, and he'll find a buyer in under an hour. But he has no idea how to organize a party."

"Good thing he has me, then." I smile and rise to leave. "I'll need fifty grand."

"Fifty grand for a party?"

"It may end up being closer to seventy-five, but let's start with fifty for now."

Luca

I fire another round into the target across the field, testing the weight as well as the accuracy of the scope, then put the rifle down on the makeshift table in front of me.

"It'll do," I say and turn to Bogdan. "We're taking four hundred as previously agreed."

"You can wire the deposit to the usual account."

"No deposit for the next three shipments."

"What? I don't take orders without a 20 percent down payment."

"You do now." I take out my phone and start walking toward my car. "Until I'm convinced there won't be any mix-ups of the containers in the future. That's how *I* work."

"Then you can forget about the fucking guns," he yells after me. "I'm not loading anything without seeing my money."

"It was a pleasure doing business with you, Bogdan," I say as I get into my car and dial Damian. "How's Isabella?"

"Better. I had an extremely interesting conversation with her earlier today."

"About?" I turn on the ignition, ignoring Bogdan who's banging on my window.

"It looks like your little wife may prove to be one useful asset."

"In what way?"

"She took it upon herself to organize your big party. It's going to be quite an event since she plans on spending seventy-five grand on it."

"I'm not hosting a party, Damian."

"Isa says you will." He laughs. "And she also made me spend three hundred and twenty grand."

"Are you fucking insane? On what? Wait a second." I roll down the window Bogdan has been banging on for over a minute and fix him with my stare. "Yes?"

"Only the next three shipments, Luca." He points his finger at me. "After that, we're going back to a 20 percent upfront payment."

"All right. Don't forget my grenades." I roll up the window, put Damian on speakerphone and reverse the car. "What did you do with the money, Damian?"

"Paid off Dario D'Angelo's gambling debt to the Albanians."

I had no idea Santino's son's gambling problems were so serious. Why the hell would we be paying off...? Oh. I'll be damned. "Does this mean we'll have Santino's support?"

"Yup. And Lombardi won't be a problem anymore, either."

"You bought his debt, too?"

"No. I called Orlando to let him know that we expect his 'yes', or else he may want to change a certain 'manicure appointment' in the future."

"Orlando doesn't get manicures. His hands look like they belong to a butcher."

"No. But Lorenzo's wife does. According to Isa, every second Saturday. Orlando has been fucking Lorenzo's wife under his nose for who knows how long." He laughs. "Your wife and her mother are running a damn spy network within the Family. They have someone in every capo's household. Domenico was in ours."

"That old scumbag who kept hanging around the kitchen all day?"

"Yup. Your woman is dangerous, Luca."

Indeed. And in more ways than I thought.

The moment I get home, I run up the stairs and go straight to Isabella's room, intending to give her a lecture. When I enter, however, she's not there. I turn around, about to head out in search of her in Rosa's room, when I hear the shower turn on.

"Isabella." I bang on the bathroom door. "We need to talk."

"I'm taking a shower. It can wait."

"You can shower later." I bang on the door again. "I talked with Damian. You're dropping your spy hobby starting now."

"You're welcome, Luca," she shouts over the sound of running water. "I was happy to help."

"This is not a fucking game! If anyone even suspects what you and your mother are doing, it won't end well!"

"You said you don't allow yelling in this house."

"New rules." I beat my open palm against the door. "Open the door, or I'm breaking it."

The water shuts off, and a few seconds later, the lock turns. I cross my arms over my chest, waiting for the door to open before I continue. When it does, all I can do is stare.

Isabella

"I'm listening," I say and lean my shoulder onto the doorframe, enjoying the way Luca's eyes are eating me up as they travel down my naked body.

"Cover yourself up." A muscle in his jaw ticks as he bites out his words.

"I was in the middle of a shower, and I plan on continuing after you're done with your tirade."

"Tirade?" He takes a step forward and looks down at me. "It's not a tirade, Isabella. It's an order. One that you better follow."

He's trying really hard to focus on my face, but his eyes keep wandering downward every couple of seconds.

"Or else?" I ask.

He places his palms on the doorframe on either side of me and bends his head to whisper in my ear. "Do not provoke me, Isa."

Isa? Oh, he must be really angry if he let that slip. I tilt my head up so my lips are nearly brushing his earlobe. "But I enjoy doing so," I whisper back, then lick the shell of his ear with the tip of my tongue. "Very much."

He takes a deep breath. There is a strange cracking sound to the left of me, but I don't move, enjoying the feel of having him so close. The need to lean into him, to press my cheek to his, and bury my fingers in his hair is eating me alive, but I fight it. I need him to come to me of his own accord—because he wants to and not because I pushed him over the edge into mad lust. I'm already toeing the line as it is.

Standing before him naked was a gamble. I half expected him to succumb, but he's still resisting. Stubborn, stubborn man. *What do I have to do to make you see me, Luca? Not the girl they made you marry, but the woman who's been in love with you for so, so long.* I don't have any more ammunition left. If he doesn't want me after all the things I've done to seduce him, is there a point in continuing to try?

His head tilts slightly to the side and I feel the tip of his nose touch the side of my neck. My body goes still while my heart starts thundering in my chest as I listen to his breathing. Having his body looming over mine, and not daring to touch him, makes me want to scream in frustration. *Do something, damn you!*

"Go back to your shower, Isabella," he says, then disappears through the door into his room without saying another word.

I stare at the door joining our rooms, closed now, and wonder how it's possible to hate a fixture with such passion. Oh, how much I loathe that door and everything it represents. Sighing, I lean my back onto the doorjamb and only then do

RUINED SECRETS

I notice it. The trim on the other side is askew, its upper part separated from the wall. I move closer to inspect the damage and trace the surface of the board where his hand had been with my fingertips, then head back to my shower, a wide smile plastered on my face.

Chapter Ten

Luca

I GRAB THE COUNTER IN FRONT OF ME AND LOOK UP AT my reflection in the mirror above the sink. There's something wrong with me. It's the only explanation.

Tonight, after leaving Isabella naked in her room, I got into my car and drove downtown while my dick was on the verge of exploding because of how hard it was. I planned to call an escort and just be done with it. I drove around for two hours, only to get back home and find release courtesy of my own hand in the shower. Again. Thinking about the nineteen-year-old in the next room.

Damian says I'm acting irrationally, but he doesn't understand my fear. I'm not a tender man, and my tastes where sex is concerned are not something a nineteen old girl would be okay with. If I let myself go, Isabella will probably get scared.

I always had to hold back with Simona. One time when I slipped, she avoided me for two weeks. When we passed each other around the house, she would stare at me with the look of a terrified gazelle and bolt.

I don't think I could stomach seeing the same fear in Isabella's eyes.

There's something that attracts me to this girl like a magnet, but I can't pinpoint what. It's not only her body, which is every man's wet dream—small with her tiny waist and the most gorgeous fucking ass I've ever laid my eyes on. Nor is it just her pixie face—all sharp lines and huge eyes. I can't grasp it. I have no idea what it is, but for some reason, I can't stop thinking about her. I keep trying to convince myself that this madness will pass, but it's only getting worse.

Then, there's my sick jealousy. I assigned Marco as her bodyguard for two reasons. First, because he's the most reliable I have and won't hesitate to get in front of a bullet for her. And second, because he's fifty-two. Still, every day I find it harder and harder to let her go anywhere with him alone. A few days ago, when I was heading out to meet with Donato, I saw Isabella and Marco leave. I had to make myself get into my damn car and drive off immediately or I would have called Donato and canceled just so I could take her to see Andrea myself.

I have no idea what's going on with me. When the fuck did I start losing my shit?

After washing my face, I get into bed, but sleep eludes me. I find myself staring into the darkness, wondering what I'm going to do with the little spymaster in the other room.

It's well into the night when I hear the faint sound of a door opening. Keeping my body still and pretending I'm asleep, I crack my eyes open just a little. Isabella is standing at the threshold of our connecting rooms, a blanket wrapped around her from neck to toes. She stays there for a few moments, then tiptoes toward my bed. Carefully, she climbs up and slowly lies down, curling on the empty side with her back to me.

Isabella

I wonder if Luca will be mad when he wakes up and finds me in his bed. He probably will, but I don't give a damn at the moment. I kept tossing and turning for hours, trying to fall asleep, but my eyes kept wandering to the sofa where Luca slept the last few nights. He didn't say anything when he came in that first time, just tossed a pillow on the end of the sofa and laid down. He didn't even undress. The sofa was way too small for him, and it couldn't have been comfortable, but he stayed the whole night. In the morning, when I woke up, he was gone. I could do the same, just sleep here a little bit and go back to my room before he notices me.

The mattress dips behind me and my eyes snap open, but I don't dare to move. If he thinks I've fallen asleep, maybe he won't throw me out. An arm wraps around my waist and pulls me back until I'm pressed against Luca's hard chest. He throws one leg over mine and tightens his hold, spooning me with his huge body. I can barely breathe, too shocked by his unexpected act. The blanket is the only thing separating our bodies, but I can still feel his warmth seeping into me, as well as his hard cock pressing into my backside.

He doesn't say anything, just lies still behind me. Slowly, I reach over and take his hand, moving it off my hip to inside the folds of the blanket until it rests between my legs. His fingers brush my core through the lacy material of my panties, and I suck in a breath.

"Not tonight, tesoro," he whispers next to my ear. "My self-control is barely hanging by a thread."

He starts to pull his hand away, but I hold onto it and press it harder to my pussy, tightening my legs and caging it in place. "You want to know what I think of your self-control, Luca?"

"Isa..."

"It can go to hell." I grind my ass right over his hard cock, and hear him growl.

"You are"—his hand tugs on my panties, sliding them down—"playing with fire, tesoro."

Luca presses his cock to my behind as his finger enters me. I gasp, arching back against him.

He leans into me and removes his finger. "Last chance, Isa."

"I will enjoy burning with you, Luca," I rasp, kicking my panties from around my ankles.

He throws his blanket off. It lands somewhere across the room as he tugs on the one I have wrapped around me, and it follows suit. His lips press onto my shoulder, then skim the side of my neck. I start turning toward him, but his arms come around me, hands sliding lower, between my legs.

"How many men, Isa?" he utters, teasing my clit with his thumb.

"What?"

"How many have you slept with before now?"

His finger enters me again, and I ride it as my nails dig into his forearm. "Does it matter?"

"No." A bite on my shoulder, then a lick. "But I still want you to tell me." Another bite. "Names, as well."

"I'm not telling you."

"The names, Isa."

The pressure he's putting on my clit makes me whimper, and then he curls a finger inside of me. I pant as tremors rack my body, my thighs trembling.

"I'm going to strangle them all," he says and moves his mouth to my neck, biting at the sensitive skin there.

I come with a loud moan, but he keeps massaging my pussy. My body continues to shake like I have a fever. Luca adds a second finger into me, and I gasp. He continues to press firmly onto my core and pump his fingers in and out. When I think I can't take much more, he pinches my clit, and I come again. I'm still trembling as he removes his boxer briefs and then places a kiss on my shoulder. He turns me onto my back, covers my body with his, and positions his cock at my entrance. For a second I go completely still. I can't help it. Then I force my body to relax as a combination of anticipation and fear consumes me.

Luca's head lowers, his lips landing on mine. Dear God, I've dreamed about kissing him for so long, imagining how it would feel. So much that it became an obsession. For some reason, in my mind, it always ended up as a slow, tender kiss, where he would tilt my head slightly and carefully taste my lips. Almost a chaste kiss, similar to those I had with a couple of boys I went out with. I was so wrong because there's nothing chaste about this kiss. It's hard and raw, like the man himself. Luca's kiss is him staking his claim. Threading my hands in his hair which is falling on either side of my face, I brush my fingers through the silky strands and let him possess me with his lips.

One of Luca's hands moves between my legs, spreading them wider, and the tip of his cock slowly enters me. I suck in a breath and close my eyes, my body rigid. *Relax*, I say to myself. It doesn't work. Luca stops, starts massaging my clit, then tries again. This time, *his* body goes rigid.

"Isabella?" he says into my mouth. "Is there something you need to tell me?"

I bite my lip and shake my head. "No."

"Look at me."

I do, and find him regarding me with his jaw set in a hard line. "Have you had sex before?"

I've been dreading this moment. It was a struggle to get this far because of his obsession with the difference in our ages, so I was afraid he would never succumb if he knew I was a virgin. I hoped he wouldn't notice.

"No," I utter and fist my hands in his hair to keep him from pulling away. "Please, don't stop."

He watches me, then shakes his head. Closing his eyes, he presses his forehead to mine. "Jesus, tesoro."

"Please, Luca," I whisper. "Please, don't stop."

"I could've hurt you, Isa. Do you have any idea how it would make me feel? Did you even think about that?"

I wrap my legs around his waist, opening myself even more for him, and slide my hands down his back. "Do it." I dig my nails into his skin. "Or I'll find someone else to do it for you."

Luca's nostrils flare as he stares into my eyes. I inhale to prepare for the pain, I expect him to thrust himself into me to the hilt. Instead, his hand slides between our bodies and he starts to circle my clit with his finger while his cock remains at my entrance.

The pressure begins to build inside of me, my breathing coming faster as his finger continues to tease me. Soon, I'm so crazy with the need to feel him inside me that I forget my anxiety and fear. His cock slides into me—impossibly slow—and there's a slight pinch of pain, but it lasts only a few seconds. Then, I'm engulfed by the sensation of his rhythm as he rocks into me, stretches me, fills me. It's slightly uncomfortable at first, but it quickly transforms into pleasure that consumes my whole being.

It's not just having him inside me, making me tremble. It's his body pressed against mine and his hands caressing my cheeks. It's Luca's eyes, piercing and dangerous, holding my gaze the whole time, and the tips of his hair tickling my shoulders and face. The way he grits his teeth because he's holding back for fear of hurting me. I never expected that from him. Even though he's mad for not telling him it's my first time, he's still trying not to hurt me. And that fact makes my heart swell with happiness.

With his breath fanning my face, Luca keeps rocking his body. In. Out. In again. My walls are stretching, taking more of him inside with every thrust. His hand moves up my body, grabs the back of my neck and squeezes.

"Is this what you wanted, Isabella?" he asks, then bites my shoulder.

"Yes," I choke out, "But now I want more."

Luca slides his cock out, then slams into me, hard, and I gasp as spasms begin in my core. A strange satisfaction overcomes me, and the next moment, my brain explodes into beautiful nothingness just as he comes inside me.

RUINED SECRETS

I'm bathing in the feeling of having Luca's body lying over mine when he pulls out and gets up. He disappears into the bathroom on the other side of the room for a moment, returning with a towel in his hand. Taking a seat on the edge of the bed, he cleans me up. Once he's done, he leans his elbows on his knees, and remains nearly motionless, gaze focused on the towel smeared with my blood. After a while, and without saying a word, he grabs the blanket off the floor and covers my naked body. His touch is gentle, but I can feel him pulling away as he starts putting on his sweats and T-shirt.

"Don't you dare try manipulating me again, Isabella," he says in cold voice. Not giving me another glance, he walks to the door and leaves the room.

For a few moments, I just stare at that damn door—yet another barrier he slammed in his wake—then bury my face in the pillow and cry.

Chapter Eleven

Luca

"So, we all agree with the decision that Luca Rossi is going to take over the Family?" Francesco asks.

Under Giuseppe's rule, Isabella's father was a consigliere to the don. I plan on keeping him as my adviser.

The men sitting around the table turn toward me. Donato nods first. Franco Conti follows, then Angelo Scardoni. Orlando Lombardi and Santino D'Angelo are next. It appears Isabella was right. Francesco turns to Lorenzo Barbini. Lorenzo looks up at me, seeming outwardly relaxed, but I notice the way he's clenching his jaw. Prior to Giuseppe's death, I was reporting to him and to the don. From this point forward, he will be my subordinate. It doesn't happen often that a capo takes over the Family. By appointing me as his successor, Giuseppe basically declared that he didn't find his underboss fit for the role. It must be a hard pill to swallow, but with five other capos in agreement, Lorenzo has no other choice. He nods.

Francesco comes to stand before me, and bends to place a kiss on the back of my hand. As a consigliere, he is the first one to swear his loyalty.

"Don." He nods and returns to his seat.

As an underboss, Lorenzo is next. He approaches with his spine rigid and his face set in hard lines, but he bends and kisses my hand. The capos follow one by one. When everyone is once again seated, I lean back in my chair and regard them.

"I heard there were some discussions regarding branching out into the drug business," I say and fix my gaze on Lorenzo. "It won't be happening. We're keeping the same setup we had under Giuseppe. Donato and I will keep handling the gun deals and laundering the money through real estate. Lorenzo, Orlando and Santino are staying in the gambling business, with Franco laundering their income. Everyone will be reporting to Lorenzo, no changes there, either."

I turn toward the young Scardoni. He's barely twenty-five and only recently became a capo following the death of his father. "Angelo, you will work with Franco and set up more businesses we can use to launder the money. We're running close to the limit with what Franco and Damian can process."

He nods.

"If I ever hear that you've set foot in Mexico again," I continue, "or that you've met with Mendoza's men, you're dead."

"Yes, Boss."

I turn my gaze to the other men around the table. "I don't want any more problems with the Russians. Next week, I'm meeting Roman Petrov to assure him we will keep the truce the Bratva agreed to with Giuseppe. Petrov let the fuckup that Bruno created slide because he knew Scardoni's deal was outside the official channels. But he won't do it again." I look at Francesco. "How much money did we lose during the three-month war with the Russians earlier this year?"

"If we include the infrastructure damaged or lost, a little over seven million," he says.

I curse. "No more quarrels with the Russians. Unless you want to see one of your daughters or sisters married off to the Bratva."

After everybody nods, I rise from the table. "That's all."

Isabella

I open the notes app on my phone and look up at Damian. "Do you want me to hire private security for the banquet, or will you have your own men in place?"

"We'll have our men at the gate and inside the house. Hire ten people to patrol the grounds, just in case."

I make a note in my planner. "I'm meeting the catering people today to pick the cake and decide on the menu. Do you have wine preferences?"

"Nope. Take whatever they think will work best with the menu," he says and looks up from his laptop. "Luca upgraded your security detail. You'll have two bodyguards from now on. Marco and Sandro."

"It would've been nice if he informed me about that himself," I mumble.

Three days. He's been avoiding me for three days, ever since I sneaked into his room. I barely see him. If I do, it's usually only during breakfast. He goes out and returns well after midnight. There must be a lot to handle since he took over as Don, in addition to his own business, but still. I considered resuming with my daily visits to his office, but have decided to wait a few more days.

"He's busy," Damian says.

"Of course, he is."

"And extremely agitated. Care to share what the hell is going on with you and Luca?"

"Why do you think it has anything to do with me?"

"Please. I know my brother better than he knows himself. You're the only person who ever riles him up so much." He starts chewing on the end of his pen. "I wonder how you do it. Luca doesn't lose his shit that easily."

"I told him if he doesn't want to sleep with me, I'd find someone who will." I shrug.

"Interesting. So, you two had sex, I take it?"

"Yes. Now he's avoiding me."

"I told you not to push him."

I put the organizer on my lap and cross my arms. "I'm done being treated like a flower arrangement in this marriage, Damian."

"You don't seem like a delicate flower to me, Isa."

"Because I'm not. And it's time your brother realizes that." I press my lips together and look back at my notes. "What about the music?"

"Anything but jazz. Luca hates it."

"How unfortunate." I smile.

"You're mean." Damian laughs. "Remind me never to get on your bad side."

"I don't usually have a bad side, Damian. Apparently, it only surfaces when your brother's around."

"You know, sometimes I don't get you two and all this drama. Why can't you act like mature people and have a normal relationship instead of circling around one another in this cat and mouse game? There's more than enough shit to deal with without it."

"I couldn't agree more. Hopefully, Luca will get the memo." I stand up. "I'm off. If you change your mind about the wine, call me."

I leave Damian's office and head downstairs to look for Marco just as Luca comes through the front door. He looks me up and down as I pass the foyer, his eyes focusing on my behind. I barely managed to squeeze into these white skinny jeans. With the way my butt is straining the material, they might not be appropriate for a business meeting. I don't give a fuck. I've been feeling like crap for days and wanted to doll up. They're my favorite pair, and they go amazingly well with my beige top and nude heels. After everything that's happened with Luca, I needed a moral boost.

"Where are you going?" he asks.

"I have a meeting with the catering company," I say and head toward the kitchen. "Have you seen Marco and Sandro?"

Silence stretches for a few heartbeats before he barks out, "I'm taking you."

I stop and turn around. "I thought you were busy."

"You thought wrong. Go upstairs and change."

"Why?"

"You won't be wearing those in front of people." He saunters over until he is standing right in front of me and nods at my skinny jeans.

"Can you be more specific? People as in strangers or..."

"Anyone but me. Is that specific enough for you?"

I raise my eyebrows. "They're jeans."

"Extremely tight jeans. Go find an oversized shirt and put it on. Or change the pants. Whatever."

"Why?"

"I don't want men ogling your ass."

"Well, my ass is rather huge, it's hard to miss." I laugh.

"Your ass is a fucking piece of art." He bends his head until his eyes are level with mine. "And it's only mine to look at, Isabella."

I blink at him. A piece of art? And only his to look at? "Are you jealous?"

His lips press into a tight line as he regards me while that vein of his keeps pulsing on his neck. "No."

"Perfect. Then it shouldn't bother you what I'm wearing and who ogles my ass," I say and turn toward the front door, intending to head to the car. Luca's hand shoots out and grabs me around my waist, pulling me to him.

"Go. Change," he whispers into my ear.

My breath catches and I close my eyes, trying to compose myself. He's finally started showing some reaction to me, which means we're getting somewhere, but he still hasn't touched me intimately since the night I gave him my virginity. The stubborn mule is still fighting it.

"If you want me out of these jeans, Luca," I say and lean back into him, feeling his hard cock at the small of my back, "you'll have to remove them yourself."

Luca's breath fans the skin on my neck as he tightens his hold around my middle. "What did I tell you about trying to manipulate me, Isa?"

Grinding my teeth, I turn and look up at him, this stubborn man who just won't let me through his shield no matter how often I hit and slash at it. I wonder if it'll always be like this between us. When will I finally be able to stop hiding the feelings I have for him? I've suppressed them for so long, they want to burst out of my chest. I reach up and hook my finger into his hair tie, pulling and releasing his hair so that it spills down and around his face. He doesn't say anything, just regards me as I tilt my head up until the tip of my nose touches his.

"You're so damn stubborn," I whisper, "but I will keep banging at this fucking wall you set between us, Luca, until it crumbles into dust."

His fingers get a hold of my chin, tilting it slightly until my lips are almost touching his. "You may not like what you'll find lurking behind that wall, tesoro," he says, his breath teasing my lips.

"Oh? But what if I do?"

The phone in Luca's pocket rings. He doesn't stop looking into my eyes as he takes it out and puts it to his ear. "What?"

I don't hear the reply from the other side, but it must be something serious because Luca suddenly straightens, his hand falling away from my face.

"I'll be there in an hour," he says and cuts the call. "I

have to go. Reschedule the meeting with the catering company for tomorrow. I'll be taking you."

"All right." I nod as butterflies flutter in my chest.

He watches me for a few moments, and I hold my breath, my eyes focused on his lips. Instead of kissing me as I'd hoped, he turns and walks out the front door, leaving me to stand in the middle of the foyer, clutching his hair tie in my hand.

Luca

I am done, I say to myself as I'm driving down the highway. Fucking *done* with pushing Isabella away, trying to stifle this mad need to grab her every time I see her, to envelop her in my arms and never let her leave my side. As soon as I get back home, I'm throwing her over my shoulder and fucking her senseless the moment we get inside the bedroom. *Our bedroom*. Starting tonight she'll be sleeping in my bed. *Our bed*. I'm calling my mission of waiting for her to turn twenty-one a failure. I can't keep her at arms length anymore. And I fucking don't want to. We're turning a new leaf, everything else be damned. Tonight, when I get home, everything will change.

I'm exiting off the highway onto a narrow road and driving uphill when I notice two black SUVs in my rearview mirror, taking the same turn. The route leading to the warehouse where we keep heavy weaponry is usually deserted. There's nothing around for miles except a few abandoned factories, so seeing two cars following me immediately raises a red flag. My hand slips inside my jacket, freeing my gun from the holster. I put it on the dashboard so it's within reach and maintain my speed. There's an intersection in about a mile, and I decide to wait and see if they'll turn off or stay on this road. I pass the crossroads. The SUVs stay on my rear and start speeding up, closing in on me. The road continues uphill, with a rockface on my left and a ravine on my right. The only option I have is to keep driving forward. There are no other intersections for miles.

That call was a scam. A setup. There was no explosion like the guard said. Looks like someone wants me dead. I floor the car.

I manage to keep my distance for a couple of miles, but the SUVs start gaining on me after that. A shot rings out. Then several more. I throw a look in the rearview mirror and spot the passenger of the nearest vehicle leaning out of the window, aiming his gun at my tires. Another shot echoes. Trying to shoot back is not an option, there are too many bends in the road. The best course of action I have is trying to lose them. A couple of more miles, then the road will start going downhill and get wider. I'll have more options for maneuvering there. Another shot. The car swerves under me. Fuck. They've hit one of my tires.

I fight to maintain control of the car and manage to straighten it, but then one of the pursuing vehicles rams me from behind, making my car lurch forward and lose traction, throwing the vehicle into a sideways skid. With a flat tire, there's no way I can escape them, so I hit the brakes, managing to stop just before I reach another curve in the road, and grab my gun. I have my hand on the door handle, intending to get out and start shooting when the other SUV rams into the side of my car. The last thing that I see before my car tumbles down the ravine is the glaring face of a man I haven't seen in years.

Isabella

"I'm not sure we can risk having the banquet outside in September. I'll order some tents to be placed on the lawn," I say as I motion for Damian to pass me the salad bowl.

"Tents?" Rosa squeaks. "So, it will be a camping party?"

"No." I laugh. "These are just white party tents. They're not for camping. They'll just provide cover in case of rain or shade from the sun."

"Oh. Can I go anyway?"

I look at Damian, but he just shrugs. "You have to ask your dad," I say. "If he's okay with it, then you can come. But you'll still be able to see everything from your window, even if you have to stay inside."

"Can I invite Clara? We can watch it together?"

"I don't see why not. There'll be a huge cake." I wink.

"Did Luca say where he was going?" Damian pipes up. "I've tried calling him, but he's not answering."

"No. Someone called earlier, and he said he had to go. I don't know who it was, but it sounded urgent. Maybe he's in a meeting and turned off his phone?"

"Luca never does that."

"Will there be a band?" Rosa asks. "Or a DJ?"

"I've hired a jazz band."

"Oh no, that's boring. And Dad hates jazz."

"I know." I laugh at the same time as Damian's phone rings.

He looks at the screen and takes the call. A moment later he abruptly gets up from his chair. For a few seconds, he just listens to the person on the other end, his face going ghostly white, then nods.

"We're coming right away," he says and disconnects the call. "Rosa, go to your room."

"But I haven't—"

"Now!" he shouts.

Rosa jumps up off her chair and dashes upstairs as I stare at Damian. I've never heard him raise his voice.

"We have to go." He takes my hand and starts pulling me with him across the entry hall toward the front door.

"Damian? What happened?"

"There's been a crash. Luca's car went off the road and into a ravine," he says, and I stumble as my heart stops beating.

"Is he . . . alive?"

"Barely."

There's a piercing pain in my chest as if someone has thrust a knife into me. As soon as we get into Damian's car, he hits the gas. I'm finding it hard to breathe, so it takes me a few tries to form the words. "How bad?"

"Head trauma and second-degree burns."

"Burns?"

"His car caught fire. I don't know anything else."

I watch the road in front of us, trying to control the urge to scream.

The smell of antiseptic and medical supplies infiltrates my nostrils. People quietly talk around us. Someone is crying in one of the rooms. The sound of my heels clicking on the tiled floor echoes as we run down the corridor. Every single thing I see and feel gets tangled up in a mess of sensations. All I can make out for sure is Damian's hand squeezing mine as he drags me behind him, his long legs covering the distance much faster than my own. A man in a white coat comes around the corner and heads toward us.

"How is he?" Damian chokes out when we reach him.

"Mr. Rossi suffered significant trauma to his head. We managed to get the swelling under control, but we won't know if there will be any lasting damage until he regains consciousness."

I grab Damian's forearm and ask the doctor, "When do you expect him to wake up?"

"It's hard to say until he's out of recovery. He might end up perfectly well, or there may be serious long-term effects."

Damian is sitting on a chair next to me, talking with someone over the phone, but all I can do is stare at the wall in front of me. We've been here for twelve hours now. Luca came out of surgery an hour ago, but he's still in the recovery room.

"They finished processing Luca's car," Damian says. "The car was totaled, but there's some evidence that the scratches and dents on the side and rear may have happened before he crashed."

I stare at him. The preliminary report said Luca lost control of the car and slid off the road into the ravine, rolling twice. It was pure luck that a fire truck was passing by and noticed his wreck and the fire. "What does that mean?"

"It means someone pushed him off the road. Based on the tire marks, probably two vehicles. Looks like someone may have rear-ended him, while another vehicle hit his side."

My heart skips a beat. Someone tried to kill my husband.

Part Two

"After"

Chapter Twelve

Isabella

Present

I slowly approach the hospital bed where my husband is lying, numerous wires hooked up to his body and connected to a machine on the right. My hand grips the bed rail to prevent my legs giving out from under me, and I nearly collapse into the nearby chair. Most of his head is tightly wrapped in bandages, they must have shaved his hair. I press my hand to my mouth to keep the sobs from escaping.

I don't know why that detail hits me so hard. I managed to keep it together while he was in surgery and during the hours he spent in the recovery room. I've put on a stoic mask and pretended I wasn't falling apart while his life was hanging in the balance. Somehow, I managed to get through it without spilling a tear.

I reach for his hand and entwine our fingers, and dropping my forehead onto the mattress, I cry. Minutes pass. Maybe hours, I'm not sure. Different scenarios roll around my mind, each worse than the one before, and I weep harder until my whole body is shaking.

I almost miss the tiny twitch of fingers in my own. My head snaps up, and I find two dark brown eyes watching me.

"Oh, Luca . . ." I choke out, then lean over him and place a light, quick kiss on his lips.

He doesn't say anything, just keeps looking at me. When he finally speaks, the words that leave his mouth make me go ice-cold.

"Who are you?"

I stare at him.

Luca cocks his head to the side, regarding me with his intense, calculating gaze.

"I'm Isabella," I whisper. "Your . . . wife."

He blinks, then looks away at the window on the other side of the room and takes a deep breath.

"So, Isabella," he says and turns to me. "Care to tell me who I am?"

I take a slow deep breath, trying to suppress the panic rising in the pit of my stomach. It's hard to know how long he was unconscious in the car, and then there were hours of surgery. It's perfectly normal for him to be slightly confused.

I place my hand over his, noticing the way my fingers shake. "I'll go find the doctor. He said to call him the moment you wake up. Okay?"

After he nods, I turn around and walk to the door, trying my best to appear calm. In reality, I'm choking down the urge to run in search of the doctor, yelling for him to come right away. When I find Dr. Jacobs, he rushes to Luca's room, asking me to stay outside. I sit in the chair and wait. And wait. I'm not sure how long the doctor has been inside when Damian comes and joins me.

When the doctor finally exits the room, we both jump from our chairs and stare at him.

"Physically, Mr. Rossi is good," Dr. Jacobs says. "Taking into account the seriousness of his condition when he arrived, I would say he's doing exceptionally well. I did a basic exam, and all his motor functions seem to be working quite well. We'll do a more thorough examination, of course, and another CT scan to make sure the swelling continues to recede, but other than some bruises and burns, he seems fine. Except for his memory loss."

I stiffen next to Damian. "Is that . . . permanent?"

"I don't know. He could wake up tomorrow and be his old self. Or it may happen in six months. Or his memory could come back in pieces."

"Does he remember anything?" Damian asks.

"He knows where he is, as well as which month and year it is. He can list the main cities, solve math problems, and he can read and write. When I asked him about some landmarks here in Chicago or elsewhere, he described how to reach them in great detail. But he doesn't remember anything personal. He doesn't know his name or recall any family members. He can't tell me the names of any childhood friends, and he doesn't know where he lives or what he does for a living."

Dear God.

"We have good psychologists here." Dr. Jacobs continues, "Once we get him out of the ICU, they can help him deal with this problem, and also give you guidelines on how to support him."

"So it might help him remember?" I ask.

"No. It will help him manage the situation. Only time will tell if he'll recover his memories."

"Okay," I say, then turn to Damian and grab his forearm. "Take the doctor to the side," I say in Italian. "Explain to him that under no circumstances is he to share the information about Luca's memory with anyone. He needs to leave it out of the reports. You'll need to threaten him. Make sure he understands that if he shares this info with anyone, he won't live long enough to regret it."

"And if he declines?" Damian asks, in Italian, as well.

"If he declines, he'll need to be dealt with right away."

Damian stares at me like he's seeing me for the first time. "I've never killed anyone, Isa. I deal with the finances. Luca is in charge of . . . the rest."

I take a step forward and look him right in the eyes. "Do you have any idea what will happen if this comes out? If anyone suspects that Luca is unfit for his . . . position, he's as good as dead. No one, other than you and me, can know."

Damian just gapes at me. He knows very well how things work in Cosa Nostra. If the don is not capable of doing his duty, he needs to step down. If he doesn't, someone will kill him in a matter of days.

"We have to tell Rosa," he says.

I take a deep breath, hating myself for making this decision, then shake my head. "No. She may slip in front of her friends. This is too big. We can't risk it."

"How the fuck do you plan on keeping this hidden, Isa? Luca doesn't remember who he is. How will he lead the Family? There are business meetings. He has Lorenzo coming to report to him every week. There are—"

"We'll figure it out," I say and squeeze his forearm. "Luca's memory will come back in a couple of days. Go talk to the doctor."

Damian leads the doctor to the side, speaking to him in hushed tones. The doctor watches him with a grim face. I hope to God Damian can convince him to keep his mouth shut. The alternative, the good doctor will have to die. I'll do whatever it takes to protect my husband, which means if Damian can't kill him, I'll have to. The thought of killing another human being has never crossed my mind, and I get lightheaded just from the sight of blood. But if saving Luca's life means I need to take another's, I'll do it.

Luca

I regard the woman sitting on the edge of my hospital bed, holding a tablet in her lap. The screen shows a photo from some event I don't remember. She turns it toward me, pointing at the people, telling me their names, roles, and sometimes even the names of their pets.

Isabella. My amazingly beautiful and very cunning young wife, who's been spending hours stuffing information in my head to make sure no one realizes that I don't remember shit.

Every morning she comes to see me, trying to fill the blank spaces in my brain with pieces of my life. My brother, Damian, always arrives around noon and takes over, vomiting business information at me, describing how I act in certain situations, and explaining who does what in both our legitimate and Cosa Nostra dealings. He leaves around three, probably to take care of tasks I should be doing, and Isabella resumes teaching me what I should already know.

She's all business when it comes to my reeducation. At first, I thought she was doing this for her own benefit because maybe she's afraid of losing her status as the don's wife if anyone finds out and decides to remove me from the position. But when I get one of the small details right, she smiles in a way that makes her eyes twinkle, and I'm not so sure anymore.

"Okay, let's go through the house staff again," she says and tries to hide a yawn.

I reach up to remove a strand of hair that's fallen over her face, hooking it behind her ear, and she goes still. Slowly, she raises her head and looks at me, surprise in her eyes. One thing I've noticed, and it has been baffling me from the beginning, is the fact that during the whole six days she's spent here, she hasn't once tried to touch me. Is it because we don't have that kind of relationship? She told me that ours was an arranged marriage. Or is it something else? Whatever the reason, I don't like it.

"That's enough for today," I say. "Go home and rest."

"You're being released in the morning. We need to go over the staff one more time."

"Security, first shift. Marco, Sandro, Gio, Antonio, Emilio, Luigi, Renato. Sergio and Tony at the gate. House staff: Grace and Anna in the kitchen. Maids: Martha, Viola..." I keep listing the names until I cover both shifts, all thirty-two people. "We're good, Isabella."

She stands, wearing a smile that doesn't quite reach her eyes. "Okay. I'll get going, then."

As she turns to leave, I wrap my hand around her wrist and wait for her to face me. "Is everything okay?"

She looks down at my hand holding her forearm, then up until our gazes meet, and nods. Her eyes flick to the side of my head. The doctor removed my bandages this morning, revealing a long, partially healed incision that starts behind my ear and curls down toward my neck. Isabella notices me watching her and quickly looks away.

"Is it that awful?" I ask. It didn't look that bad to me when I inspected it in the mirror after the doctor had left. Only six stiches.

"What?"

"The scar?"

"No, it's just . . ." She lifts her eyes to mine, reaches up with her hand, and lightly brushes her fingers over the hair tied at the top of my head. "I was worried they had shaved it all off," she says in a strangled voice.

"Just the bottom part." They got rid of everything below the crown, leaving the rest.

"I like it. Very stylish." She plays with one of the strands that has escaped the bun.

I was rather surprised when I realized I had long hair. I didn't expect that for some reason and considered cutting it. But after seeing that it makes her happy, I decide I'm keeping it.

Isabella leans forward to look at the back of my head, and a faint vanilla fragrance envelops me. I turn my head, burying my nose in the crook of her neck, and inhale. She tenses but doesn't move away, just steadies herself a little more and sighs.

"Did your family make you marry me, Isabella?" I ask and cup her cheek with my hand. "You're way too young."

"No."

"Then why did you marry me?"

She doesn't reply right away, just nuzzles my neck with her nose for a few moments. "Because I'm in love with you, Luca," she whispers, then goes rigid, like she didn't mean to say those words.

"And me? Am I in love with you?"

Isabella steps away and smiles. "Of course you are," she says and brushes my cheek with the back of her hand. "I have to go. Don't forget to call Rosa."

"I won't," I say.

I've been calling Rosa twice a day, in the morning and in the evening. She'd usually be the one who talked while I mostly listened. About her friend Clara who has a cat. About the construction workers who came to fix the façade and one of them ending up in the rose bush. About movies she watched. It has been the hardest thing so far—talking with my child without having any recollection of her. Almost as hard as shaking my head when Isabella showed me a photo of a dark-haired girl with shoulder-length hair, asking me if I recognized her.

I don't remember my daughter.

"Damian and I will be here first thing in the morning," Isabella says and leaves the room without looking back.

Chapter Thirteen

Isabella

I stand next to Damian in the hospital hallway, staring at the door as we wait for Luca to come out of his room.

Dear God, what the hell possessed me yesterday to tell him he was in love with me? I spent the whole night awake, trying to think of a way to correct that fuckup. What kind of person am I, lying to a man who's lost his memory about something so important? I didn't mean to say it. It just kind of burst out of me. I was so fucking scared this whole week, worrying that Luca's condition may change for the worse, or that someone from the Family may make an appearance and find out about his memory loss, that I wasn't thinking straight and just blurted out that nonsense. So, now what? Should I come clean right away? Or wait until we get home?

The door opens, pulling me from my internal turmoil, and Luca comes out, dressed in a dark gray shirt and black pants. I think he's lost a couple of pounds during his stay, but it's barely noticeable. He still looks the same—larger than life.

After a few words with Dr. Jacobs, Luca nods at Damian, and then his eyes land on me. I offer him a small smile and turn toward the exit when I feel his arm around my waist.

"Is something wrong?" he asks.

"No. I'm just nervous."

"Don't be." He bends and whispers in my ear, "You've taught me well."

He kisses me on the top of my head, and I close my eyes, swallowing the tears that threaten to spill. This lie will probably make me burn in hell, and Luca will most certainly hate me when he finally remembers everything. But walking down the hallway with his arm around my back feels so right, and the heart in my chest literally makes a leap. That kiss. The way he watches me with affection instead of reluctance. His warmth next to my side. I've wanted this for so so long. I don't want to go back to the cold treatment. Not now, when I almost lost him. As we leave the hospital and walk toward the car, I make my decision.

I'm not telling him the truth.

As we pull up to the house, and Damian parks the car, I nod toward the man standing at the front door. "Emilio." I tell Luca. "The one at the gate was Tony."

"Emilio. Tony." He repeats.

"Rosa's waiting for us inside."

Luca grinds his teeth and nods. "How . . . how do I call her? Do I have a pet name for her?"

Something squeezes in my chest upon hearing his

question. "You call her 'piccola,'" I choke out and take his hand in mine.

"And you?"

I blink in confusion. "Me?"

"Yes," he says and passes his free hand through my hair. "Do I have a pet name for you as well?"

I bite my lip, and stare into his eyes, then whisper. "You sometimes called me 'tesoro.'"

Luca nods and leans forward. "Thank you, tesoro."

"You're welcome." I choke out, barely able to keep my emotions at bay.

When we enter the house, I face Luca and force a smile. "Welcome home." I place my palm on his chest, raise onto my tiptoes, and place a quick kiss on his chin. "Viola by the stairs. Martha on the left," I whisper. "Ask Viola how her son, Fabio, is doing."

We move toward the stairs, the maids watching us approach. They dip their heads slightly, a welcome home to Luca.

"Mr. Rossi, it's good to have you back."

"Thank you, Viola. How's Fabio?" he asks.

"Better, Mr. Rossi. His leg is healing fine. Thank you for asking."

Luca nods and places one hand on the stair railing when the sound of running feet reaches us.

"Dad! Daddy!" Rosa shouts, running toward us across the foyer.

Luca turns just in time to catch her as she throws herself into his arms, and I watch Luca's face, holding my breath. My hope that seeing Rosa would trigger something in his brain and help him remember quickly fades when Luca turns to me with a haunted look in his eyes. I hold utterly still, carefully schooling my features. He still doesn't remember his daughter.

"They wouldn't let me visit you in the hospital!" Rosa weeps, clinging to his neck. "I was so scared."

"Hospitals are not places for kids, piccola," Luca whispers, gently holding the back of her head with his bandaged hand.

"Did they really open your head? Uncle Damian said they did and had to patch it back together with iron nails because your head was too thick for them to sew it."

"Well, you know your uncle is an idiot. Don't listen to him."

"I knew it." She laughs. "Can I see?"

Luca turns his head to show her, and Rosa makes a disgusted face. "Yuck, Dad. That's nasty. And what's with the hipster haircut? You're too old for that. Isa, did you see this?"

"Yup," I say and notice Luca watching me. "I love it."

"I have to go. Clara will be here in fifteen, and Grace is making us a cake." Rosa kisses Luca's cheek. "Love you, Dad."

"I love you too, Rosa."

She dashes off to the kitchen. Luca stares after her with a somewhat shuttered look in his eye, and my heart squeezes. How do you deal with the fact you don't have any recollection of your own kid?

I open the door between our rooms and peek inside. "Luca?"

For a second, panic rises in my stomach. What if something's happened? The doctor said they did a thorough evaluation, and with the exception of his memory loss, every other test came back with positive results. Still, I'm constantly on edge. The sound of running water in the bathroom reaches me, and I exhale in relief.

"Luca?" I cross the room to the en suite. "Is everything . . .? What the fuck are you doing?"

His head is under the tap and he's reaching for the shampoo bottle on the counter. "Washing my hair," he states the obvious.

I grab the shampoo. "Are you out of your fucking mind? You have second-degree burns on your arm. Dr. Jacobs said you can't let the bandages get wet."

"You curse quite a lot when you're mad."

I curse again, squeeze a bit of shampoo onto my hand and start lathering his hair, making sure I don't let the water reach the back of his head. Rinsing takes quite some time because he has a lot of hair, even with a fair bit of it shaved off.

"Don't move." I open the cupboard to grab a clean towel, then proceed with drying his hair. Luca doesn't say anything through the whole ordeal, just regards me with a strange look in his eyes. When I'm done, I comb through his hair and turn around to look for a hair tie, but there isn't one in sight. I take off mine and gather Luca's hair, securing it at the top of his head. "All done."

He straightens, caging me with his arms against the counter, and slowly bends until we're at the same eye level.

"Do you sleep here? In this room?" he asks, and I tense. "Yes."

Luca smirks and cocks his head to one side. "Then tell me, Isabella, why aren't any of your clothes in the closet?"

Shit. I should have thought of that. The way he watches me, with his eyes staring right into mine like he can uncover all my secrets with one look, is highly unnerving. "Because I have a lot of stuff." I blurt out "I'm using the wardrobe in the room next door."

"Hmm." He lifts his hand and places it under my chin. "Tomorrow morning, I'm having Martha and Viola move your clothes in here."

What? Why? "Sure. Anything else?"

"Yes." He tilts my head up a bit more. "I prefer your hair like that."

"Down?" I ask and he nods. "Thank you. Consider your preference noted."

He narrows his eyes at my comment. Did I miss some meaning there? I'm not sure how to act around this new Luca because he's not behaving like he used to.

"I'm going to take a shower," he says. "Are you coming?"

My breath catches. God help me, but I like this new version of him so much better. "Yes."

Luca

My wife is hiding something. What it is, exactly, is a mystery, but it has something to do with our relationship. I went through every part of the bedroom and each piece of furniture when I came in here, and I didn't find a single thing of hers.

Isabella removes her dress, then her bra and panties, and my breathing stills. She's an amazingly beautiful little thing. I let my gaze travel down her firm little breasts and narrow ribcage, then from her tiny waist to her generous hips and shapely legs. She has the body of a fucking goddess. "Turn around," I rasp and barely manage to keep my hands to myself when she does. Even though I don't remember shit, I'm sure my eyes have never landed on a more perfect ass.

"Now you." She turns to face me and starts unbuttoning my shirt. When she's done, I remove the shirt and throw it next to her dress on the floor. The rest of my clothes follow soon after.

"You lost some weight," she says, placing her hand on my chest.

"How much?"

"A few pounds." Her palm slides down my stomach and then moves to my hip. "Five, maybe six."

I checked the chart at the hospital. I lost six pounds since being admitted. She knows my body well, and still, something feels off. Based on how comfortable she is with being naked around me, I'm fairly certain we've had sex before, so it can't be that. *What are you hiding from me, Isabella?*

Her touch leaves me as she gets into the stall. For a few moments, she fumbles with the shower head, adjusting its position, then turns on the water and looks up. "Keep your arm out of the spray."

I join her inside. Isabella watches me, but keeps her eyes focused on my face instead of my hard cock, pretending she doesn't notice it. We both know where this is leading. It's been inevitable from the moment she started removing her clothes, but we keep dancing around it. She lathers her hands with soap and presses her palms to my chest, massaging, and it takes tremendous self-control to keep myself from reaching out and grabbing her. Somehow, I manage and close my eyes instead, enjoying the sweet torture as her hands travel across my chest and then down, but when I feel her fingers brushing my cock . . . well, my patience hits its limit.

"Enough." I turn off the water, reach out and press my palm to her pussy. Slowly, I slide a finger inside. Isabella gasps but doesn't pull away, her huge eyes glued to mine. Smiling, I slightly curl my finger inside her.

"Hands on my wrist, Isabella," I say, "and don't you dare let my finger slip out."

I wait until her hands wrap around my wrist. With my palm cupping her pussy and finger still buried inside of her, I take a step back, pulling her with me. It takes us a couple of minutes to leave the bathroom and reach the bed, step-by-*tiny*-step, and by the time we do, Isabella is panting, but she doesn't let go of my hand.

I move to stand behind her, press my chest to her back and bend my head to whisper in her ear.

"On the bed," I say and slide another finger inside her. "Slowly."

Isabella lets go of my wrist and starts crawling toward the middle of the bed. I follow, hunched over her, keeping my fingers buried in her.

"Stop." I wrap my left arm around her waist, ignoring the pain the strain inflicts on my burned skin. "I'm going to remove my fingers now," I say next to her ear.

"Please, don't." She presses her legs together and moans.

"Don't worry." I place a kiss on her shoulder. "I'll be only a second, and then I'll make it better."

"Promise?"

"I promise." I kiss her neck next. "Front? Or from behind?"

"Front."

Isabella whimpers when I slowly slide out my fingers, then turns onto her back and hooks her legs around my hips.

I just watch her for a few moments. Her hair is tangled, her mouth slightly open, and her chest rises as she pants.

"Please, Luca."

I want to take her in one hard thrust, but I felt how tight she is. So, instead, I place the tip of my cock at her entrance and slide in just a bit.

Isabella growls in displeasure and digs her nails into my back, pulling me closer. My little wife—always so composed and calm—just growled at me. Our eyes lock, and I crush my mouth to her lips, thrusting all the way inside. She gasps but doesn't close her eyes, watching me.

"You like the feel of my cock filling you up, don't you, Isabella?"

"Yes." She breathes out, then squeezes her legs around me.

I slide out, then drive into her again, hard. "How much?"

Isabella doesn't reply, just moves her hands up my back and pulls the hair tie from the knot at the top of my head. My hair falls, framing my face, and she threads her fingers through it as her body arches up. I pull my cock out, press my fingers over her pussy, and start teasing her clit. Her hands in my hair grip the strands, pulling, and it takes a lot of control not to bury myself inside her again.

"I asked how much, Isabella?"

"So, so much." She gulps air with a hiss. "I wish it could stay inside me all the time."

An answering growl rumbles from my throat as I slide back inside her. When I bury myself to the hilt, a sigh of relief leaves her lips. My God, I can definitely get behind the idea of having my cock buried in this woman. Permanently.

The bed squeaks under us as I pound into her, soaking up her every grunt and sigh.

The need to take her from behind is growing too strong to ignore. "Turn around," I say and slide out.

Isabella turns and rises onto all fours, perching her ass. Holy Mother of God, I almost come from just seeing that perfection. I grab her around the waist and bite her right butt cheek. Then I slap that sweet ass twice in quick succession. A yelp escapes her, then another one when I bury my teeth in her other ass cheek. Moving my hands around her hips to her front, I find her clit and tease it as I thrust my cock inside. I feel her walls gripping my length. Moaning, she lowers her head to the pillow, raising her ass even higher, and I lose it completely. I begin to thrust faster into her sweet pussy, then smack her ass cheek again and watch as my handprint appears, marking her. Gripping her hips, I continue my punishing pace. A muffled scream leaves her when I slam into her and her inner walls grip my cock, the sensation causing my orgasm to hit me before I'm ready to be done with her. Still, I can't help but relish the feel of my seed pouring inside, branding her.

Isabella's body is still shaking when I pull out and lie down next to her. With my hand around her waist, I bring her against me, pressing her back to my chest, then slide my hand across her front until I cup her pussy with my palm.

"Don't even think about moving." I whisper into her ear and keep my hand covering her pussy. "I want my cum in you the whole night."

Slowly, I slide one finger inside and Isabella sucks in a breath.

"I don't know how we've slept before," I say, "but this is how we'll sleep from now on. Is that clear?"

She nods and glides her palm down my forearm and lower until she covers my hand and presses it, pushing my finger deeper.

"If your hand is anywhere else when I wake up," she says, "I'll be very displeased, Luca."

Isabella

When I open my eyes next morning, Luca is sitting at the edge of the bed, unwrapping the bandage from his left arm.

"The doctor said you should go to the hospital to have your bandages changed," I say.

"No time. I'm going to the office with Damian. We need to be there in an hour."

"You were discharged less than twenty-four hours ago. Maybe you should take a few days off."

"I don't remember shit, Isabella. I need to get up to speed on my own life. There's no time to waste."

"You say that as if you don't believe your memory will return."

"Dr. Jacobs said it might happen in months. Or years. Or never. I don't plan on sitting at home and hoping for a miracle that may never happen," he says.

"That's a very... pragmatic way of looking at the things."

He tilts his head and looks at me sideways. "Do I have a choice?"

"No. I don't think you do." I crawl over the bed until I'm sitting behind his back and place my chin on his shoulder. "Is it bad?" I nod at his arm.

"Not so much," he says and looks at me from the corner of his eye. "Don't faint."

"I never faint," I say as he unwraps the last of the bandage and removes the dressing.

"Dear God, Luca." I suck in a breath and quickly bury my face in his neck. The skin on his arm, from just below the shoulder all the way to his wrist is mottled red, and looks like it was scrubbed raw. "Do you need help?" I mumble into his neck.

"No, I'll manage."

He starts putting some kind of balm over the burns on his arm, but his movements seem too sharp, and he's rubbing the sensitive skin way too much.

I slide to the edge of the bed next to him and take the jar. "Let me do it."

I'm not good with blood or wounds of any kind, but the rough way he's going about it will only make it worse. Taking a deep breath, I scoop a good amount of the balm with my fingers and carefully start applying it to his wounds, first focusing on the less damaged parts. Then, I move up his arm, leaving the worst of the burns to be treated last. Not a very wise decision. When I come to his bicep, my hand is shaking so much that I have to pull away for a moment to calm myself. I don't want to risk hurting him more. Luca's hand wraps around mine, and he moves it back to his wounded skin.

"You're doing great," he says.

I nod and resume applying the balm, trying my best to be as gentle as possible. When I'm done, I place a thin piece of sterile gauze over his damaged skin and bandage his arm. Only then do I let myself sag.

"I'm sorry," I say and close my eyes. "I don't deal well with this kind of stuff."

His hand cups my face and a kiss lands on my lips. "I think you deal quite well with anything that gets thrown at you, Isabella," he says against my mouth. "Unexpectedly well, I might add."

"Not really." I kiss him back. "I'm just good at pretending."

"Are you pretending now?"

"No."

"Good. I don't want you pretending with me." His lips move across my cheek, toward my ear. "But I know you're hiding something from me, Isabella," he whispers.

My eyes snap open. "I'm not hiding anything."

"Yes, you are." He bites my ear slightly and stands up. As he walks toward the wardrobe I enjoy the view of his powerful body moving with grace. Watching Luca move around has always been one of my favorite things, but I usually had to do it in secret. Being able to do so freely feels strange. I still can't believe he's finally mine. Well, at least until he remembers he doesn't like me. Then, he'll probably hate me for lying to him. But I don't care. It will be worth it.

Chapter Fourteen

Isabella

I PLACE MY FIST TO MY FOREHEAD, SWITCHING MY GAZE between Luca and Damian every few seconds. We're fucked.

"I don't have the slightest idea, Luca." Damian raises his hands in the air and sighs.

"How the fuck am I going to discuss the next shipment with the Romanians if I don't know the terms we agreed to?" Luca asks.

"Well, you'll have to improvise."

"Do you even know what we ordered?"

"Not a clue. I just launder the money you throw my way. You're in charge of everything else. I don't know the quantities, the rates, or the payment terms."

"What about Donato?" I throw in. "He should know most of that stuff. You just need to find a way to wring the info out of him without actually asking."

"I'll take him with me,"—Luca nods—"say I'm planning

on passing the reins over to him since I'm busy with the Family shit, and that I want to see how he'll manage."

"That could work. What about trying the goods?" Damian asks. "Do you remember how to assemble and shoot your toys? Because Donato only knows how to handle his own gun. Barely."

"Yes."

"Good. That leaves us Orlando Lombardi as the last pressing issue for now. Everything else can be dealt with without a face-to-face meeting. At least for now."

"What about him?"

"He's throwing a party for his son, Massimo. He just turned eighteen, and the party is on Wednesday. You two are invited." Damian points his fingers to me and then Luca. "And everyone will be there."

"You're not going?" Luca asks.

I place a hand on Luca's arm. "He's persona non grata in the Lombardi household. At most of the Family households, actually. He wasn't at our wedding for the same reason." I smile and look at Damian. "He was sleeping with Constansa, Orlando's youngest daughter, while in a relationship with the older one, Amalia."

"You were fifteen when that happened!" Damian widens his eyes at me. "How do you even know about that?"

"When Orlando caught him in Constansa's room, he had to escape through the window," I add. "Everyone talked about his naked ass running across the garden while Orlando chased him with a shotgun."

"I had my boxer briefs on, for God's sake." Damian rolls his eyes.

"Any other love affairs I should know about?" Luca asks.

"We should go over the real estate business one more time." Damian answers, pointedly ignoring Luca's question.

"Damian."

"All right, damnit, I'll make you a list." Damian waves his hand dismissively and opens his laptop. "Let's go through the real estate we sold this month and what we'd like to consider purchasing."

I lean back on the sofa and watch Luca as he listens to Damian dumping heaps of information on him—details on money laundering schemes, commission rates, numbers, rental terms, explanations of agreements they have with the biggest clients he may end up meeting. They already covered people at the office while Luca was in the hospital, but Damian goes over their names and roles one more time. Luca doesn't speak much, only asks a question here and there, and keeps listening, absorbing. I don't know how I would deal with this if it were me in a similar situation. I'd probably lose it after two days. But not Luca.

The other day, Damian found a video from a reception held last year for the real estate businesses. Luca spent the whole morning watching a two-minute segment where the camera caught him, studying the way he moved and talked. He's extraordinary. It's been ten days since he came back from the hospital, and he hasn't slipped once.

When Luca told me Lorenzo was coming by to update him last Friday, I was scared shitless. Trying to fool the second most important man in the Family is not the same as deceiving the household staff. Damian and I did our best to fill him in on everything they could potentially discuss, but our knowledge was limited. Still, Luca pulled it off, somehow.

We have three days until Massimo's birthday party, not

nearly enough time to go over everyone we might meet there. I'll have to start combing social media and downloading images of people I haven't shown him so far.

"If you two don't need me, I'm going to find Rosa," I say and rise off the sofa. "She wanted to buy new curtains for her room, and I promised I would take her."

I head toward the door, but as I'm passing Luca, he stands up, grabs me around my midriff, and pulls me against him.

"I'm coming with you," he says and slides his hand to my butt.

"We have work to do, Luca," Damian barks from his spot behind the desk.

"It can wait."

I look up to find Luca watching me. Based on the glint in his eyes, he's interested in something other than picking out curtains. Smirking, I slide my hand under his shirt and brush the tip of my finger across his lower back. We had sex twice this morning—in the bed first, then in the shower—but it was rather quick since Luca was in a hurry. I can't wait for tonight when we won't be rushed. My absolute favorite part is when he spoons me after we're both spent and sated, and slides his finger into me. It felt a little strange the first night, having his finger in my pussy while I slept, but I got used to it pretty quickly. Now, I don't think I could fall asleep any other way now.

Before the crash, he barely touched me, especially when someone else was around. He only relented when I pushed him into pleasuring me. And he only kissed me once—when we slept together that first time. His behavior has taken a one-eighty after the crash. Sometimes, I find it hard to connect this Luca with the one from before.

Luca

"Didn't we come for curtains?" I turn to Rosa, who's browsing the bed throws.

"I'm too old for a pink room. I want to change everything," she says and picks a faux fur cover in a shade of gray. "I love this! Can we get it?"

"If we have to." The thing looks like a yak hide.

"Yes! I'll see if they have cushions to go with it."

"We should buy one for our room," Isabella adds.

I look down at her, placing my hand under her chin, and tilt her head up. Big brown eyes meet mine and she laughs. Jesus, she is so beautiful.

"No dead animals. Real or fake," I say.

"You're no fun."

"Oh?" I squish her to me, pressing her into my body. "We'll see about that tonight."

"Well, I see you're up and about," A high-pitched voice exclaims behind me. "I thought you were half dead."

Keeping my hand around Isabella's waist I turn around to look over at the blonde woman standing a few paces away. I remember her from the photos Isabella showed me. "I'm sorry to disappoint, Simona."

She narrows her eyes at me and then looks down at my arm around Isabella. Damian only briefly filled me in on my first marriage because we were more concerned about business-related details.

"I'll come to pick up Rosa on Thursday," she says, and Isabella lightly squeezes my waist once, then one more time.

"No," I say.

"No?" Simona sneers. "You can't keep me from seeing my child."

"You get Rosa on the weekends," Isabella says.

"I don't remember asking you anything."

"Enough!" I snap. "You will not talk to my wife in that tone. Are we clear?"

"What? She was—"

"Are we fucking clear, Simona?"

She scrunches her nose at me and tilts her chin, but shuts up.

"Rosa will be ready at ten on Saturday," I say and look down at Isabella. "Let's go find Rosa and check out those glasses you said you liked."

I walk toward the other end of the shop until I'm sure we're well out of Simona's earshot, then glance at Isabella. "You need to fill me in on my relationship with Simona. Damian only told me I have full custody, and that she takes Rosa a couple of times a month. Why did we divorce?"

"She was supposed to be in Europe till the end of the month, so we thought it wasn't the most pressing matter," she says and cocks her head. "Damian will have to be the one to fill you in on Simona and her issues. He knows much more, and anyway, I'm not a fan of your ex, so I'd prefer not to discuss her."

"Why not?"

Isabella arches her eyebrows. "Isn't that obvious? She had you first, and I hate her for that."

I take a step forward and place my hand at the back of Isabella's neck. "What about your exes?"

"What about them?"

"Who had you first, Isa?" I take another step forward, then one more, making her walk backward until her back hits a wall. Her eyes regard me without blinking, and the corners of her lips curve up.

"I already told you that, Luca," she says and smirks. "Before."

"You know I don't remember." I slide my hand into her hair and tug. "Tell me."

A knowing smile spreads over Isabella's face as if my frustration amuses her. I grit my teeth and bend until my face is right in front of hers. "Speak," I bite out.

She raises her hand and grips my chin, still wearing that smug smile. "You," she whispers and presses her lips to mine. "It has always been only you for me, Luca."

"Good." I bite her lower lip and slide my palm down her back to the waistband of her skirt. It's one of those with an elastic waist. How convenient. "Can you see Rosa?"

Isabella's breath hitches when I slide my hand under the waistband of her skirt and squeeze her butt cheek. "She's . . . at the cash register," she chokes out, looking behind my back to the opposite side of the store. "Waiting in line."

"How many people are ahead of her?"

"Five."

"Perfect." Beneath her skirt, I move my hand to her stomach and dip it lower, between her legs, pressing over her pussy.

"Luca," Isabella whispers. "There are people here."

"I know." I place my free hand on the wall next to her head, move her panties to the side and position my finger at her entrance. She's already wet. "Take a slow, deep breath."

She blinks at me, then inhales, and my finger enters her at the same moment.

RUINED SECRETS

"Good?" I ask.

Those big brown eyes watch me with intensity, then grow wider when I push in even deeper.

"I asked you something, Isabella." I bend my head to bite at her earlobe lightly.

"Yes," comes her barely audible answer.

I slowly remove my finger, then slide it back inside. An adorable little moan leaves her lips. Her breathing quickens as I fuck her with my finger. Based on how my hand is completely drenched with her juices, she's close.

"And now, how many people before Rosa?" I ask as I curl my finger.

Isabella takes a deep breath then tilts her head to take a quick glance behind me. "She's next."

"What a shame. Looks like we'll have to finish at home."

Isabella's hand grips my wrist. "Don't you dare," she says through her teeth.

"You want to come here?" I whisper next to her ear. "With all these people around?"

"Yes," comes her breathy answer.

I smile and thrust my finger inside her, pressing onto her clit with the heel of my palm. Isabella moans and comes all over my hand.

Chapter Fifteen

Isabella

The bedroom door opens, and Luca comes in, carrying a thick folder with a bunch of papers inside.

"You stayed late today," I say.

"Yeah. And I have homework as well." He drops the folder and his jacket on the recliner next to the bed and bends down to me. Holding my chin between his fingers, he places a quick kiss on my lips. "What are you reading?"

"Economics."

He raises his eyebrows. "I'm going to take a quick shower and come join you. We can read our shit on economics together."

When he disappears into the bathroom, I try to get back to my reading, but my mind keeps wandering back to that quick kiss. So casual. Natural. He called me his wife that morning at the furniture store. In front of Simona. I think it was the first time he's ever called me that. And it felt so good.

Will everything change when his memories return? Will he go back to his old, detached self? I've never thought about myself as a selfish person, but in this moment, I realize I am. Selfish, greedy, and mean. Because somewhere deep inside me, there's a poisonous seed of hope that he'll never get his memory back. And I am utterly disgusted by that realization.

Ten minutes later, Luca comes out of the bathroom, his hair is loose and he's wearing gray sweatpants, and a white T-shirt. Laid-back looks good on him. Well, everything looks good on Luca. The burns on his arm seem to be healing well. The skin is still red, but looks much better than it did when the bandages were removed.

Luca sits down next to me, leans back onto the headboard, and wraps his arm around me. "Come here."

He pulls me to him until I am sitting between his legs, with my back pressed to his chest. Then, he leans over and picks up the folder he left on the recliner and places it on the bed next to him. I open it and skim over a bunch of numbers on the first page. "Cash flows?"

"Yup," he says as he reaches for his jacket. He takes a pair of glasses from the pocket and puts them on.

I stare at him.

"What?" he asks and grabs the first piece of paper.

"You wear glasses?"

"For reading, apparently. I found them in a drawer at the office today, and the numbers started making much more sense when I could see them clearly." He tilts his head and narrows his eyes at me "You didn't know your husband needs glasses?"

"My husband never told me," I say, then lift my hand and thread my fingers through his hair. He looks hot in glasses. "I guess the cat is out of the bag now."

"Hmm. You and your husband had a really strange relationship, Isabella." He leans in and kisses me.

Oh, Luca, you haven't the slightest idea of how much. I brush the back of my hand over the side of his face, then take my book and lean back onto his chest. Not five seconds later, his right hand slips under my silk nightgown and into my panties. He places his finger at my entrance and slowly slides it in. I gasp and look over my shoulder to find him focused on the cash flow printout in his left hand, seemingly immersed in the numbers.

"Luca?"

"Yes?" he mumbles, not looking up.

"I can't concentrate with your finger inside me," I state what should be obvious.

"Well, too bad. Because it's staying there, Isabella."

"You expect me to be able to read like this?"

He finally looks up from his report, his face the embodiment of seriousness. "You'll get used to it. I enjoy having my fingers inside you, so every time you sit next to me, that's where they'll be. Do you have a problem with that?"

I blink at him. "No."

"Perfect." He nods and turns back to his papers.

"What if there's someone else around?" I ask.

"In that case, I may reconsider."

He may reconsider?

With the book on World economy in my hands, I try to ignore his warm palm over my pussy and his finger inside me. It doesn't work. I know how skilled his hands are, and it's driving me mad. Trying to keep the rest of my body still, I slowly squeeze my legs together. Luca's still engrossed in the report as I start rotating my hips just a little, enjoying the feel of my walls brushing his finger.

"Isabella."

I don't stop but turn my head and find him regarding me over the rim of his glasses.

"What?" I arch an eyebrow.

"Behave."

"And what if I don't wish to behave?"

Luca tsks, lets his papers fall to the floor, then takes the book from my hands and launches it across the room. "Take your clothes off."

"You first," I say. "But keep the glasses."

A deep rumble leaves his lips. When he grabs the hem of his T-shirt to remove it, I can't help but sigh at the sight of his biceps bulging in the process. I get a hold of his sweatpants, but a second later end up on my back, with Luca holding the hem of my nightgown.

"Not the silk one!" I shout, but it's too late. He's already tearing the material. That's the fourth one this week. "Damn it, Luca!"

While he's removing his pants and boxer briefs, I take off my panties so they don't meet the same fate as the nightgown. When I look up, I find Luca regarding me with hooded eyes.

"You're so fucking sexy," he whispers, grabs me around the waist and pulls me to him. "I want you to ride me, but don't you dare come until I say you can."

Wetness pools between my legs.

"Why?" I straddle him and press my palms on his chest, positioning myself above his fully erect cock.

His hands grab at my butt cheeks, squeezing. "Because I said so."

I bite at my lower lip and lower myself, taking his thick length inside of me inch by inch. "And what if I can't control myself?"

Luca tilts his head up and snags my chin, his eyes staring daggers at me. "You will."

I smirk. There's something unbelievably sexy about him ordering me around, especially when he wears those glasses. "If you say so, Mr. Rossi."

The moment the words are out of my mouth, I feel his cock twitch. I lower myself until I'm fully seated in and rock my hips, already close to coming. Luca lifts his hand to my lips and pushes his thumb into my mouth. I suck on it in the same rhythm as I move my body while the pressure in my core builds.

I glide my palms up his hard chest and rock my hips, enjoying the way my walls stretch to accommodate his size. As I reach his hair, I sink my hands into his dark strands, making sure I don't accidentally touch the wound on the back of his head. They removed his stitches last week, but I'm sure it still must be sensitive.

"Why are you so fixated on my hair?" he asks as he trails his hands down my back, the rough skin of his palms causing goose bumps with his every touch.

"I'm not," I breathe out, then lean down to nip at his chin.

"You keep taking the elastic out every time you have the chance, Isabella." His hands travel down to my ass. He lifts me and slams me back down onto his cock. "Why?"

"I like seeing your hair down, that's all," I say.

The truth is, it makes me feel special. Luca never wears his hair loose in public. Before his accident, I only saw him with his hair unbound a handful of times, and it always felt as if I got a glimpse of something forbidden. I'm so crazy in love with him that I get excited by something as inconsequential as the fact that he now almost always removes his hair tie when we're alone.

I straighten and grind against him, enjoying the sight of him under me.

"Don't you dare come." Luca says through gritted teeth and squeezes my ass.

I smirk.

Suddenly, Luca grabs me around my waist and lifts me up until he's holding me just an inch above his cock. I wrap my hands around his thick forearms and bury my nails in his skin, glaring at him. The devil just smiles.

"Frustrated looks good on you, Mrs. Rossi," he says and lowers me a bit until the tip of his cock enters me. I try moving down so I can take all of him back inside me but fail. Leaning forward, I fix him with my gaze and move my right hand to his hard length. Then, I squeeze it. A deep rumble leaves Luca's mouth and the next moment I find myself lying on my back, with his big body looming over mine. He gathers my wrists into his right hand and moves my arms above my head, keeping them locked there.

"Now, you can come," he says and slams into me with such force that I scream and come instantly. He keeps pounding as I ride my orgasm until his seed spills inside me.

Chapter sixteen

Luca

"Camilla, Orlando's wife," Isabella whispers as we walk across the room at Massimo Lombardi's eighteenth birthday celebration.

"She's the one who's addicted to sleeping pills?"

"Nope. That's Lorenzo's wife, Ludovica," she says, then continues with the rest of Orlando's family. "Next to Camilla are his daughters Constansa, the taller one, and Amalia. Don't mention Damian in front of them."

From the way Isabella is holding herself—pressed to my side, her arm tightly wrapped around mine, whispering in my ear with a smile on her face—people will probably presume we're having a very private conversation. Her feet must be killing her in the heels she's wearing. She purchased them yesterday, specifically for this occasion. The damn things are more than five inches tall, but she said it was necessary because of our height difference. Even with the added inches, I still need to bend my head to hear what she murmurs.

After a short talk with Orlando, we take drinks from a passing waiter and move toward the corner of the room. Several people approach us along the way, and thanks to the hours I've spent with Isabella going over photos and videos, I recognize most of them. For a few, I have trouble connecting the faces to names, so I discreetly squeeze Isabella's waist and she jumps into the conversation, giving me hints. It's astounding how she manages to make it look so natural. Unforced.

Lorenzo stands on the other side of the room with a red-haired woman and a few men I don't recognize. They weren't in the pictures Isabella showed me. The woman seems familiar, but it takes me a few moments to recall her. Lorenzo's wife. She's changed her hair. She was blonde in the photos. Lorenzo looks up and our gazes connect. I'll have to speak with him later, or it may come across as suspicious. Lorenzo has been the biggest challenge so far since neither Isabella nor Damian could fill me in on all dealings I've had with him.

A man in his late fifties starts heading our way from across the room, a woman in her early thirties on his arm.

"Franco Conti. Second wife, Ava," Isabella says into her glass.

One of the capos who's in charge of laundering the money from gambling, I recall.

"Damian said you haven't met his wife yet. She wasn't at our wedding," Isabella adds before they reach us.

"Franco." I nod. "I see you finally decided to let us meet your wife."

After the introductions, Isabella starts chatting with Ava while Franco stands beside me, watching the crowd.

"I'm concerned about Angelo," he says. "I'm not sure he's fit for the role you gave him."

"Why?"

"Numbers are not his forte."

I look around at the grounds, pretending that I'm thinking about what he said while I'm trying to filter through the plethora of information in my brain. Who the fuck is Angelo? I squeeze Isabella's waist lightly.

"Angelo Scardoni is here?" she exclaims next to me. "I wanted to ask him about Bianca and how she's doing with being married into the Bratva."

Oh, yes. The youngest capo whose sister married the Bratva's enforcer a few months back. I forgot his name.

"He will have to learn," I say, having no idea what role I assigned him. It probably has something to do with the money laundering.

"Did you talk with Lorenzo?" Franco asks.

"About?"

"He was extremely . . . unhappy when you vetoed his drug business idea."

From what Damian told me, we have never dealt in drugs. Damian mentioned that Angelo Scardoni's father tried something behind the old don's back, and it didn't end well. I can't recall all the details. "Lorenzo's happiness is not my concern," I say.

"Are you sure that's wise?"

I turn to him, making certain my face shows what I think of his impromptu question.

"I apologize, Boss." Franco quickly looks down.

"If you overhear Lorenzo mentioning his idea again, to anyone, you will let me know."

"Of course." He nods and takes his wife's arm. "I'm glad to see that you're well. The Family was worried."

"They have no reason to be."

When Franco and his wife leave, I look down at Isabella and find her holding her phone, texting someone. I step behind her, wrap both of my arms around her waist, and rest my chin on her shoulder. "Who are you texting?"

She looks at me sideways, her eyebrows raised. "Why?"

"Is it a male someone?"

"Yes."

"You won't text any men unless they are related to you by blood." I lightly squeeze my arms around her and growl into her ear. "Or I'll kill them, Isabella."

"Jealous?" Her lips curl in a barely visible smile.

"You have no idea how much."

"I'm texting Damian. There are some people here we didn't expect, and I need him to let me know if there's any important information you should know."

"My little scheme master." I drop a kiss on her exposed skin.

Isabella goes still. "You shouldn't do that, Luca."

"Kiss you?" I let my mouth travel upward to her neck and kiss her again. "Why?"

"You're not exactly known for displaying affection around other people. Especially not at the Family gatherings."

"Too bad. I enjoy showing everyone you're mine."

"Everybody already knows that, Luca. Most of them were at our wedding."

"They might know,"—I turn her so she's facing me—"but I want them to see as well."

Holding her around the middle, I lift her off the ground and press my mouth to hers, as a surprised little yelp leaves her lips. She doesn't kiss me back right away. I've probably shocked her. The thing is, I find myself rather surprised by my act as well. I never intended to make a scene, which is exactly what I'm doing based on the dumbfounded looks on the faces around us, but I couldn't resist this unexplainable urge to claim her in front of everyone. Maybe because I saw other men watching her, their eyes skimming every part of her that's on display in that skin-tight burgundy dress.

I bite her lower lip lightly, and Isabella finally starts kissing me back, slowly at first, but then, her hands wrap around my shoulders and the nape of my neck, and her kiss becomes greedy. That's much better. I feel something wet on my face and open my eyes to find Isabella's eyes still closed but tears rolling down her cheeks.

I gently lower her back down and take her chin between my finger and thumb. "Tesoro? What's wrong?"

She presses her lips together tightly and shakes her head, her eyes still closed. More tears fall from them.

"Too much pressure. Stress," she says. "Don't mind me."

She sounds sincere. I don't believe a word. "I'm taking you home."

"Yeah. Let's go through the garden." She opens her eyes but avoids looking at me. Instead, she nods toward the balcony door. "I don't want anyone witnessing my breakdown."

"Okay," I say and take her hand in mine, leading her outside.

Something's wrong. I might have lost my memories, but I haven't lost my mind. She will tell me what the fuck I did to make her cry in front of fifty people. Because, even though I can't say I've known her long, one thing I'm completely sure about is the fact Isabella would never let the members of the Family see her cry.

Isabella

I sag into the passenger seat and exhale. Shit. Luca walks around the front, sits behind the wheel, and starts the car.

"Feeling better?"

"Yeah." I nod, open my clutch and retrieve a small mirror and tissues to clean the mascara marks from under my eyes. Waterproof, my ass.

"Care to tell me what just happened there, Isabella?"

"I already told you. Stress overload." I keep wiping my cheek with the tissue but the black stains just won't come off, damn it. "Just forget it."

The road ahead of us is free of other vehicles, but Luca slows down and then turns into a gas station parking lot. In the rearview mirror, I notice the car with our security detail make the same turn, and park a few spots away.

"Why did you stop?" I ask.

Luca doesn't say anything, just leaves the car and heads toward the building. One of the security guys exits the other car, but Luca motions with his hand for him to get back inside. A couple of minutes later, he returns and drops a package of wet wipes onto my lap.

I look at the package, then up at my husband, who sits with his elbows on the wheel, staring through the windshield. Slowly, I take a wipe and proceed with cleaning my face. "Are we waiting for someone?"

"Yes. For you to start talking, Isabella."

"Jesus Christ." I throw the used wipe into my purse and close the small bag. Why won't he just leave it alone?

As far as I'm concerned, we can stay here all night because there's no way I'm telling him I was so fucking affected and happy to have him kiss me in front of everyone. Like I matter. Like I have dreamed of him doing for so long. Like . . . he's in love with me. Just to realize that he probably did that only because he believes we're a couple happily in love. Before, he didn't even find it fitting to kiss me on our wedding day.

"I have nothing else to say. Can we please go home?"

"All right." He starts the car.

The thirty-minute drive passes in complete silence. When we arrive, Luca parks in the driveway, and comes around to open my door. He still doesn't say anything. Maybe it's better this way. Tonight has been exhausting, and I'm not in the mood to fight with him. And on top of it, my feet have been killing me for hours. So, prior to getting out of the car, I take off my heels and hold them in my hand as I head toward the house. I take maybe three steps before Luca scoops me into his arms and carries me toward the front door.

He doesn't put me down when we get inside, as I expected, but proceeds to climb the two flights of stairs. Inside our bedroom, he lowers me onto the bed, then turns around and disappears into the bathroom. A few seconds later I hear the shower turn on.

Instead of waiting for him to finish, I hurry into my old room and take a quick shower there. When I leave the bathroom, I look at my old bed, then at the door between the rooms. I don't want to sleep alone, but maybe it would be better to avoid more questions, so I shut the adjoining door.

Turning down the covers, I get into my old bed and snuggle under the blanket.

I've just closed my eyes when a loud bang makes me spring up. I search for the source, and my eyes land on Luca standing in the doorway between the rooms. He's completely naked, his hair is loose, and by the look on his face, he's angry as hell. The door next to him is hanging askew by only one of its hinges.

"It wasn't locked, damn it!" I snap.

He stalks over to the bed, grabs me just under my ribcage, and hauls me up. Then, he throws me over his shoulder.

"Really mature," I mumble as he carries me to our bedroom. When we reach the bed, he deposits me onto it, then lies down over my body, holding himself on his elbows. Caging me in.

"You sleep in this bed," he says through gritted teeth. "Nowhere else. Is that clear?"

"Even when we have a fight?"

"Even when we have a fight, Isabella."

"Okay," I say, brushing my fingers through his hair. It's ridiculous how soft it is, I could spend the whole night just passing my hand through it.

"What did I do to make you cry?" he asks and bends his head. "It was the kiss, wasn't it?"

"Luca..."

"Did you feel uncomfortable because people saw us kissing?"

I gape at him. "Why would I?"

"Because I'm so much older than you, and you find it awkward to kiss me in public. Why didn't you tell me?"

"What?!" I stare at him with wide eyes, wondering how the hell he came to that conclusion. "Of course, not!"

"Don't lie to me, Isabella. I want the truth."

He wants the truth? Fine. I take his face into my hands and look directly into his eyes.

"I've been in love with you for years. Years, Luca," I say. "I lived for those short moments when you'd come for a meeting with my grandfather. I basically stalked you around the house, hiding behind furniture or bushes in the garden, just so I'd get to look at you."

I squeeze his face, then continue.

"Before we got married, every night for two years, I fell asleep only after pleasuring myself and imagining you were next to me. I've never been with any other man except you because, even when you were off limits, I didn't want to sleep with anyone else," I say and kiss him. "I've loved you for as long as I can remember, Luca. And being kissed by you in front of the whole Family was my dream come true. I cried because I was happy."

"So you don't think I'm too old for you?" he asks, staring down at me.

"Luca, baby, I don't give a damn how old you are. I've never wanted any other man in my whole life."

Luca's hand cups my jaw and he watches me through narrowed eyes for a few moments. Then, he slides his hand down and under my nightgown to cup my pussy. "No one's had this except me?"

"I already told you, you were my first." I tilt my head and kiss him again. "In fact, you're the only man who has ever touched it."

His body goes still above mine, and for a few seconds,

it looks like he isn't even breathing as his eyes bore into mine. And then he snaps. Grabbing the hem of my nightgown, he pulls at the silky fabric until a tearing sound follows. My panties meet the same fate soon after. If this continues, I'll need to shop for new underwear every week. Or stop buying it all together.

He presses his right hand to my pussy and teases my clit while his left hand travels down my body, trailing from my neck, across my chest and stomach, until it's between my legs, too. His eyes never leave mine while he slides his finger inside me, still massaging my clit with his other hand.

"Only mine," he whispers and adds another finger, making me gasp.

A self-satisfied smirk pulls at his lips. He slides down and buries his face between my legs, replacing the finger on my clit with his tongue. My breathing hitches as the pressure in my core keeps building, but just as I'm on the brink, he removes his hand. I whimper at the loss of his fingers, then moan when he sucks on my clit and almost come undone. As I'm about to go over the edge, his mouth vanishes, too. I stare frustratedly at him as he looms over me, his eyes narrowed.

"If I find you in that other bed ever again, you won't like the consequences," he says. "Do you understand, tesoro?"

I tilt my chin up and smirk. "And what will you do?"

Luca leans forward, the corners of his lips curling upward in a wicked smile. He slides his finger inside me again, painfully slow. I grab at his hand, pulling on it with all my might, trying to get his finger to move faster without effect. He just smiles wider, then pulls his hand away.

"Luca!" I get a hold of his wrist and pull his hand back between my legs.

"Yes?" He presses the tips of his fingers to my pussy, pinches my clit, then removes his hand again. I feel like I'm going to break from frustration.

"Please," I whimper.

"If you ever dare to sneak out of my bed again," he says and bites my earlobe, "I'm going to torture you for hours. Understood?"

"Yes."

"Good girl," Luca whispers into my ear, then buries himself to the hilt inside me.

My breath hitches and I pant as he rocks his hips, filling me up more with each thrust. I grab at his upper arms, squeezing, enjoying the sensation of his muscles flexing under my palms. The pressure at my core builds and when he slams into me with a roar, I shatter.

I'm still shaking when Luca slides his cock out and grabs me around the waist, turning me around.

"Have I ever told you how obsessed I am with your ass?" He squeezes my butt cheeks and scrapes his teeth across the skin, then bites.

"Maybe once or twice," I breathe out, then moan when he licks the spot where his teeth had been.

"Every time you enter a room and my eyes fall on your sweet ass, I have the urge to tear your clothes off you and do this," he says and his cock enters me again.

Grabbing onto the sheet, I widen my legs a little more, then gasp when he starts pounding into me. His hand slides down my side and across my lower belly. He rocks his hips while his finger finds and teases my clit. I can't get enough air in my lungs as he continues to hammer me from behind. My walls start spasming around his length while my arms and legs shake uncontrollably. When he buries himself fully, his seed filling me, I moan and come again.

"You're shaking like a leaf," Luca says as he lies down next to me and pulls me to his body. "Are you cold, tesoro?"

"I don't know," I mumble and nuzzle my face into his chest. My whole body is trembling, but I think it's the aftereffects of having two of the most amazing orgasms, one right after another.

"Here." He covers us with a blanket. "Better?"

I tilt my head up and nip his chin lightly. "Yes. But you forgot something."

"Oh? Did I?" He slides his hand down until he reaches my pussy and brushes the tip of his fingers over my folds. "What might that be?"

I bite his chin again, then turn around so that my back is pressed to his chest. "Don't keep me waiting," I say.

His palm cups my pussy, and I take a deep breath in anticipation. Nothing happens.

"Luca!"

"Yes?" I feel his breath at my nape. "Do you need something, tesoro?"

"You know I do."

"Tell me."

Oh, how he enjoys torturing me. I place my hand over his between my legs and press on it. "I can't fall asleep without your finger inside me, okay?"

It's slightly embarrassing to confess, but it's the truth. Last night he was going over some Family matters with Damian, and they stayed in his office until well after midnight. I spent the whole day with the catering company and was dog-tired, but when I went to bed, I couldn't sleep. I tossed and turned until Luca joined me somewhere around two a.m., and only when his finger slid inside of me did I manage to fall asleep.

"I know," he whispers into my hair and pushes his finger into me. I suck in a breath. My pussy is still sensitive, but when his finger is seated fully in, the feeling of comfort washes over me. I sigh, close my eyes, and fall asleep.

Chapter seventeen

Isabella

There's a squeak of the closet door, followed by some rustling. I open my eyes just a crack, squinting at the sunlight coming through the window. Luca is standing by the bed, putting on his pants.

"What time is it?" I ask.

"Half past seven. I'm taking Rosa to buy some things for school. I don't want to wait until later. It will be madness the closer it gets to the end of summer. After that I'm driving her to Clara's. They'll be camping in the backyard."

"Have her take a jacket. It may rain today." I turn over so I'm on my stomach, fold the pillow, and prop my chin on it so I can still watch Luca. "I'm seeing my sister later. Are you coming back for lunch?"

"Probably not. I have a meeting with Franco Conti at noon, and after that, another sit down with the real estate agent."

"I'll have lunch with Andrea, then."

"You'll wear the blue dress today. The one that ties around

the neck," he says and pins me with his gaze. There's a challenge in his dark eyes.

I tilt my head to the side, watching him. What an odd way to say it. Not "Will you wear the blue dress for me?" or something similar, and he knows I've noticed.

"Okay," I say and watch as his eyes flare. "Can I wear the nude heels with it?"

A look of satisfaction crosses his face, but it lasts just for a second before he hides it. Interesting.

"Yes." He nods and starts buttoning his shirt.

I regard him, and a realization slowly forms in my head. My, oh my . . . if I'm right, and I'm pretty certain I am, my husband has been hiding some rather interesting things about his preferences. I decide to test my theory.

"I'd like to put my hair in a bun today," I say, choosing my words very carefully, and regard him closely for his reaction. "Will you allow it?"

His fingers on the button still. Slowly, he turns toward me, and our eyes lock.

"No. You will leave it down," he says, his eyes daring me.

"Okay. Will you allow it tomorrow? Please?"

"I'll think about it." He takes his jacket off the chair, grabs his keys and wallet, and heads toward the door, but then he stops at the threshold. I see his hand form a fist like he's warring with himself about something, then turns to face me. For a few seconds, he just watches me, the knuckles on his fisted hand going white. "Starting today," he says, "I will be approving all your outfits. When I'm not here and you need to go somewhere, if you plan to change, you'll call me to approve it first," he says at last and keeps his gaze on mine, waiting for my reaction.

"Of course, Luca." I nod.

He unfolds his fist, a tiny, satisfied smile forming on his face. I wouldn't have noticed it if he wasn't facing me, but his pants tightened across his crotch upon hearing my answer. This is turning him on. As soon as he leaves, I grin and roll onto my back. I knew Luca was holding back with me, but up until this moment, I didn't grasp how much. But I do now, and I'm ready to play.

"I hear you and Luca made quite an impression at Lombardi's," Andrea says over the rim of her cup.

"How would you know when you weren't there?"

"Milene called and gave me a full report. With all the sizzling details."

"It was just a kiss." I shrug. "Nothing particularly saucy about it."

"Luca Rossi caught kissing in public? The man no one has ever seen so much as touch his previous wife? I'm amazed it wasn't covered in the morning news."

"People tend to exaggerate things," I say. "Why weren't you there? You said you were coming with Mom and Dad."

"I was grounded." She scrunches her nose. "Dad caught me sneaking out the night before."

"What?" I slam my cup down. "Alone?"

"I wouldn't have been alone. I was going out with Catalina."

"Where?"

"To a club."

"Please tell me you were going to take Gino."

"Of course not. God, I hate that guy. He acts like he's my father. And Dad lets him! Why couldn't I keep Leandro as my bodyguard?"

"Because he's too old to run after you when you slip," I snap. "You're too reckless. Sneaking out in the middle of the night. Running away from bodyguards. You need someone to rein you in, and I'm glad Gino is managing."

"He's prohibited me from going to Perla's birthday party next week!" she barks. "How can he prohibit me from anything? He is a fucking bodyguard! When I told Dad, he said he agrees with everything Gino decides."

"Where's the party?"

"At Baykal."

"You were planning on going to one of Bratva's clubs? After what happened at Ural the last time? Are you out of your mind?"

"That mess was your fault." She grins.

"You can't go to the Bratva's club! For God's sake, Andrea!"

"Kostya would have been there." She shrugs. "Catalina has been seeing him. Kind of."

"Dear God! Does her father know she's going out with one of the Bratva's men?"

"No. And you won't tell him! It's nothing serious, they're just . . . talking."

"From what I've heard, half of the city's female population have been through Kostya Balakirev's bed. He's not the type of man to just talk with a woman."

"That's not true."

"He slept with Amalia Lombardi last month. And their cook. I'm not absolutely sure, but I think he slept with Amalia's mother, as well. He's worse than Damian."

"It scares me sometimes, you know? How much shit you remember about people."

"You can never anticipate when knowing someone's dirty laundry may come in handy." I look down at my phone. "I have to call Luca. I'm going shopping with Milene this afternoon and have to change. He wants to approve what I'm wearing."

"He what?" Andrea widens her eyes at me.

"I've been unearthing some very interesting things about my husband recently." I smile. "One of them is that choosing what I wear really turns him on."

"He's controlling you?"

"No. I'm letting him control me. And enjoying every second of it."

"Isa, that's . . . kinky."

"Yeah, I guess it is." I grin and call Luca.

He answers on the first ring. "Where are you?"

"Having coffee with Andrea at my parents' house."

"Did you take bodyguards?"

"Marco and Sandro are waiting for me in the car. Don't worry."

A few moments of silence, and then, "Are you wearing the blue dress as I instructed?"

"Yes," I say. "I'm going home to change. I have some errands to do. I'll send you a picture of what I put on before I leave."

"Good. Call me the moment you get home."

"I will."

Luca

The man across the desk keeps talking, showing me and Damian images of houses and condos on his tablet, and listing the benefits and downsides of each. With a load of money from arms deals waiting to be laundered, we need to increase the number and size of the properties that pass through our company. Fast.

"We need bigger properties, Adam. And more." I throw the paper with the prices onto the desk.

My phone rings, showing Lorenzo's name. I look up at Adam and nod my head toward the door. "Leave. I'll call you later."

When the door closes after him, I take the call and put it on speakerphone so Damian can hear as well. "Lorenzo."

"One of Octavio's bookkeepers has been taking money on the side," he says. "That needs to be taken care of, Boss."

"All right."

"Do you want me to handle that?" asks Lorenzo.

I look at Damian who shakes his head, then I reply, "No. I'll take care of it."

"We're keeping him in the back room in Octavio's casino."

"I'll be there in forty minutes." I cut the call and look up at Damian. "How do we take care of thieves?"

"Kill them," he says. "You can assign someone else to pull the trigger, but Giuseppe handled thieves personally. It was a statement."

I lean back in the chair and think it over. Even though I don't remember killing anyone, the idea of taking someone's life doesn't seem to trouble me. "I'll do it. Do you want to come?"

Damian cringes. "I'd rather not. But I'll draw you a floor plan. You'll have to go inside Magna through the back entrance since they have metal detectors at the front door."

"I know."

His head snaps up. "You remembered something?"

"No. I don't have any recollection of going there or meeting people, but I do know how the inside looks."

"That's bizarre," he says and starts chewing on the pen he's holding. "What are we going to do if your memory doesn't come back?"

"We'll just keep going as we've been doing so far. I don't think anyone suspects anything."

"You don't find that possibility disconcerting?"

"It frustrates me, yes, and I hate that I don't remember my daughter or my wife. But the doctor said I can't do anything about it. And I can't waste my energy dwelling on things I can't change." I stand up and head toward the door. "Instruct Adam to search for more real estate. I'm going home after I dispose of that bookkeeper."

Getting to Magna doesn't pose a problem. I spent two days driving across Chicago with Damian, who pointed out all our businesses, as well as other locations where I may need to go at some point. I remembered everything about the city but couldn't connect the names of the casinos with any particular location until I saw it.

My phone pings as I'm parking the car in the back alley.

It's a selfie from Isabella, showing her standing in front of the big mirror in our bedroom. She's wearing a flowing brown dress with white flowers, and there is a mischievous smile on her face. Smirking, I type a quick reply. *Approved, tesoro*.

I send the message, put my gun in the holster under my jacket, and leave the car. Emilio parks his car behind mine, but I raise my hand, signaling him to wait for me here, and head to the metal door on the right. A man in a dark suit is standing by the entrance with his hands clasped behind his back.

"Boss." He nods and opens the door for me.

I walk down the long corridor and turn left, heading into the back room. It's strange how everything around me seems familiar but I have no recollection of ever being here. It was the same with my house the first day I came home from the hospital. I remembered the layout but not who had which room. It was as if someone had erased random parts of my memory and left only crumbs for me to follow.

Two men are flanking the double doors at the end of the corridor. They open it when I approach, letting me inside a medium-sized room which smells of stale booze and sweat. Lorenzo is sitting behind the desk at the far corner, but he quickly stands up when I enter. A man I don't recognize is leaning on the furthest wall, probably one of the Family's foot soldiers. I'll have to tell Isabella and Damian to dig up some photos of the soldiers for me. Until now, I haven't had time to go over the lower-ranking men in the Family hierarchy.

In the center of the room, a man in his late fifties is sitting on a wooden chair. His shirt is wrinkled and there are specs of blood on it. Based on the bruises on his face and his swollen lip, he's been roughed up a bit while waiting for me. The thief, I presume. The moment he sees me, he starts fidgeting in his chair as much as the ties around his hands and legs allow.

"Boss." The man I don't recognize nods, moves away from the wall, and stands next to the bookkeeper.

"What proof do you have that he's guilty?" I ask, turning to Lorenzo.

"We found double books on his desk. According to them, he stole close to twenty grand last month."

"You're sure they weren't planted?"

"They were in his handwriting," Lorenzo says and crosses his arms. A small smile forms on his lips. "If you want, I can take care of the thief, Boss."

Yeah, I'm sure he'd love that. I don't need Isabella and Damian to tell me that Lorenzo isn't happy with me becoming the head of the Family. I can see that quite well myself. He thinks he's hiding it well, but I've been paying close attention to everyone around me, looking for subtle tells or double meanings. A man in my position can't afford to miss anything because only one slip will be enough to initiate my downfall.

"Yes," I say and take two steps until I'm standing behind the tied-up man. "You do that."

The smile on Lorenzo's face widens as he reaches inside his jacket for his gun. He likes the idea of me being reluctant to kill a man and letting him do the job instead. Especially in front of a foot soldier. I turn, wrap my right arm around the bookkeeper's chin and place my left hand at the back of his head. One strong twist. The man's neck snaps.

I unwrap my arms from the bookkeeper's neck, then turn to face Lorenzo, who's staring at me, obviously surprised. It would have been easier to just shoot the guy, but Damian said this was supposed to be a statement.

"Make sure the body won't be found," I say and leave the room, feeling two sets of eyes boring into my back.

When I get inside my car, I dial Isabella, turn on the speakerphone, and start the engine.

Isabella

I've just finished removing my makeup when my phone rings. Luca's name flashes across the screen, and I hit the button to accept the call, putting it on loudspeaker.

"Where are you?" comes a clipped question from the other side.

"You're in a nice mood," I say as I toss the soiled wipes into the garbage. "Did something happen?"

"Seems like Lorenzo is playing games."

"It was expected. What did he do?"

"I don't want to talk about my underboss now. Where are you?"

"In our bedroom."

"Take off your clothes."

I put the cosmetics and face oil down on the dresser, remove my dress, then my underwear. "Done."

"The bed. Lie down on your back."

I smile, walk to the bed with the phone in my hand and lie down as instructed. "Okay. Now what?"

"Put your hand between your legs. You're going to stay that way and tease yourself until I arrive."

"And when will that be?"

"In twenty minutes. And Isabella . . ."

"Yes?"

"Don't you dare come before I get there."

What? "I'm not sure I can manage that, Luca."

"Well, if I find out you came earlier than I allowed, we will start again, and this time, it will be an hour instead. Do you understand?"

"Yes."

"Good. Turn on the speakerphone and leave the phone next to you."

"It's on. You'll be listening?"

"Of course. You can start."

I let my hands slide down my body to my pussy and start teasing my clit in slow circles.

"Do you know how many times I pleasured myself imagining it was you next to me?" I ask.

"Tell me." Comes a gruff answer.

I press onto my clit, then add another finger. "Are you sure?"

"Isabella."

Oh, I love when he says my name with that commanding tone. It's a request, as well as an order at the same time. Luca gives off much more emotion with his tone than with actual words.

"The first time I did it, I was seventeen." I moan and keep teasing my pussy. "I've done it every single night and sometimes during the day. So, I would say at least a thousand times."

"And what was I doing to you in those fantasies of yours?"

"You would come into my room." I smile and slide one finger inside me, enjoying the tingling and building tension at my core. "You would wear a suit. That all-black combination that makes you look both edible and dangerous at the same time. You would approach me slowly, tear off my dress, and throw me onto the bed." I place my other hand on my clit, massaging it as I push my finger even deeper, imagining it's his cock. "Then, you would bury your face between my legs and eat me out until I screamed."

"Without taking off my suit?" he asks.

"Yes." I bite my lip and pull out my finger, afraid I'll come.

"And what would I do, then?" There's a strain in his voice. I can hear it loud and clear.

"Are you hard, Luca?" I ask and press my palm over my pussy, hoping it will help subdue the need to thrust my finger back inside myself.

"Answer me, Isabella!" he barks. "What would I do next?"

"You'd place your body over me, your weight pressing me into the mattress. Then, you'd kiss me, and I would taste myself on your lips."

"Would I still be clothed?"

"Yes. I'd remove your jacket and shirt first. Your breathing would quicken as I dig my nails into your shoulders and kiss you in the center of your chest. Then, I'd help you remove your pants."

I can't take it anymore, so I slide two fingers inside myself and gasp.

"What did you just do?" he asks.

"Nothing." I breathe out and slide my fingers even deeper, moaning.

"Did you come, Isabella?" he snaps.

"Not yet," I whisper. "Are you close by?"

"I'm passing through the gate," he says. "What happens next?"

I smile and keep playing with my pussy, enjoying the

sounds of his labored breathing coming from the other end of the line.

"You'd gather my wrists in your hand and pull my arms above my head. Just like you usually do." I moan as the pressure between my legs builds. "And you would bury yourself inside me in one thrust. Hard. To the hilt."

The door on the other side of the room bangs open. Without removing my hand from my pussy, I lift my head from the pillow and look between my bent legs at the threshold. Luca is standing in the doorway, gripping the frame on either side of him, his jaw set in hard lines as he stares at me.

I take my lower lip between my teeth and start circling my clit with my free hand. My fingers are still inside me, so I slide them out and move them to my mouth, licking each one of them slowly.

"Tell me, Luca,"—I smile—"how hard does this make you?"

A deep growl comes from him. He takes a step inside, kicking the door closed behind him, and walks slowly toward the bed, removing his clothes along the way. The jacket. Then, his charcoal shirt. The pants. He's looking at me the whole time. When he reaches the bed, he is completely naked, his cock fully erect. I wet my lips and widen my legs a bit more.

"You're the sexiest fucking thing that has ever walked this earth." His voice is a low, primal rumble as he grabs behind my knees and pulls me toward him. Wrapping his arm around me, he turns me around so I'm on all fours on the bed. In the next instant, I feel him entering me from behind.

"So wet." He brushes his palm down my back. "Did you orgasm before I got here, Isabella?"

"No." I gasp as he buries himself all the way.

"Good. You're not allowed to come unless I'm here with you." He slides out, then slams back inside again.

"Am I allowed to play at least?"

"Only when I say so." Another slam, his cock filling me completely. The pressure that has been building in my core intensifies. "You do not touch your pussy unless I give you permission. Do you understand?"

I press my lips together and lower my head, my breathing coming hard through my nose.

"Do. You. Understand?" He keeps pounding into me, punctuating each word with a hard thrust making me gasp for air.

"Yes!" I scream.

Luca's rapid pounding thrusting doesn't stop. He looks at me and commands, "Come."

I scream again as the orgasm suddenly hits me. Luca groans and explodes into me.

Chapter Eighteen

Luca

My phone on the nightstand buzzes. I put my glasses on and take a look at the message from Donato, saying the gun delivery has been fucked up again. I'll need to ask Damian if he knows what happened the first time, but that can wait until I get to the office. A piercing pain jolts through my skull between my temples, and I suck in a breath. It's gone just as quickly. Maybe I should go see Dr. Jacobs for a checkup. This isn't the first time it's happened.

Isabella wriggles in my arms, then places her palm over my hand between her legs and presses on it. She certainly has become addicted to having my finger in her pussy. Yesterday we took Rosa and some of her friends to a movie. The kids sat in the first row, but Isabella and I stayed in the back. Once we were alone, she took my hand, slid it under her skirt, and whispered that her pussy needed it. The small sigh of relief that left her lips as I thrust my finger inside her made me so hard I barely managed to stop myself from dragging her off like a caveman. She fucking whimpered when I had to remove my finger at the end of the movie.

I brush the palm of my free hand down Isabella's back, squeeze her ass lightly, then run my fingers over the skin on her side. "I can count your ribs, Isabella. Have you lost weight?"

"I'm trying to slim my butt a bit. I'm on a diet," she mumbles.

"What?" I put a knuckle under her chin and raise her head to make her look at me. "Did you ask for permission to starve yourself?"

"No." She blinks at me, looking slightly confused. "I thought men liked skinny women."

"You thought wrong."

"My butt is huge, Luca. I want to be a size down before the party."

Squeezing her chin, I lean forward until I'm in her face. I don't want her ass to get smaller. I want it larger. "How much weight have you lost?"

"Ten pounds."

"You have two weeks to put that weight back on, Isabella," I say, scowling at her.

"It will all go to my ass. It will get even bigger."

An image of Isabella, with her beautiful behind a size or two larger, fills my mind and my cock swells. "Good."

"Fine." She rolls her eyes. "I guess those new pants I bought yesterday will go to waste. I barely managed to get into them as it is."

"Fuck the pants." I move my hand to her backside and squeeze her ass cheek again. Her butt does seem smaller. "I want this as it was."

"Is that an order?" She smirks.

"Yes."

The smile on her face widens. "I like when you order me around."

I curl my finger to expand the pressure against her walls and press my thumb to her clit, loving the way she squeezes her thighs together to hold my hand in place.

"It turns me on so fucking much when you wear these glasses, Luca."

I growl and keeping her flush to my body, I turn us over on the bed until she is lying under me, and lean closer to whisper in her ear. "And what else turns you on, tesoro?"

"The frustration I feel for those few seconds when your finger slides out of me during the night, just before your cock replaces it." She breathes out and mewls when I do just that, but I keep my fingers on her clit, teasing her.

"This is tyranny," she says, sliding her hands through my hair.

"I know." I bend my head to bite her neck, pinching her clit at the same time.

"Damn it, Luca!" She fists my hair.

It amuses me to no end that she gets frustrated when I don't bury my cock inside her right away. I position myself at her entrance and start sliding my cock into her greedy little pussy. God, the sounds she makes. Sometimes I think I could come simply from hearing her moans.

"Is it better now?" I retreat, then push into her.

"Yes . . . Yes . . . Yes . . ." She pants to the rhythm of my pounding into her while her body shakes under me, climbing the high. I pinch her clit again, then massage it. She squeals a little when I pinch her clit again and squeezes her legs around me.

"I love the sounds you make, tesoro." I bury myself within her with a groan. "So damn much."

She whimpers and grabs my shoulders as she comes. I thrust inside her again and explode, marveling at the feel of my cum filling her up. The best feeling ever.

"Come here." I wrap my arm around her waist and press her back to my chest. She's still trembling when I cover her pussy with my palm and slide my finger back inside her.

"I wish I could have your finger, or your cock, inside me all day," Isabella sighs.

"You don't like the feel of your pussy being empty?"

"Nope." She cocks her head and looks at me. "You've made an addict out of me."

"Perfect."

"I might need to start stopping by your office during the day. To get my fix."

"I like that plan." I smile, then nuzzle her neck. "And I'll arrange something else for you in the meantime."

"What do you have in mind?"

"You'll have to wait and see, tesoro."

Isabella

"Can I dye my hair red?" Rosa asks from the opposite side of the dining table.

"No." Both me and Damian reply in unison.

Rosa leans back in her chair and crosses her arms over her chest, her chin tucked in.

"When you grow up, you can dye your hair, sweetie," I say, "You're too young for that now."

"But I want to," she mumbles.

"Why? Have some of your friends dyed their hair?"

"Nope. I still want to do it."

I sigh and shake my head. It's exactly as if I'm listening to my sister. "How about a new haircut? I can take you next week. We could do our nails too."

Rosa's gaze snaps to me, her eyes wide. "Really?"

"Sure." I nod. "I'll call my stylist and tell her to book another spot. Do you have a specific hairstyle in mind?"

Rosa fidgets in her chair, then shrugs. "I want it short," she says, then looks up at me. "Do you think Dad would let me?"

"If you explain that you'd really like to have it short, of course he would."

There's a sound of footsteps approaching, and Luca rounds the corner, coming into the dining room.

"Dad!" Rosa jumps in her chair, "Can I cut my hair short? Isa said she'll take me with her. Can I? Please?"

Luca stops behind Rosa and places a kiss at the top of her head. "Sure, piccola. Now, go to the kitchen and help Viola with food. I need to speak with Isabella and Damian."

"I want to hear, too!"

"It's business stuff, Rosa. Go. Please."

Rosa scrunches her nose, gets up from her chair, and leaves reluctantly.

As soon as she's gone, Luca turns to Damian. "Salvatore Ajello requested a meeting," he says. "Who the fuck is Salvatore Ajello?"

I stare at Luca while panic starts gathering in the bottom of my stomach. "When's the meeting?"

"Tomorrow," he says. "Who is he?"

"The don of the New York Family," Damian says. "Do you have anything on him, Isa?"

"A ton of gossip. Nothing useful. And I don't know anyone who does." I don't think many people even know what the don of the New York crime family even looks like. If you need to contact the New York Cosa Nostra, you call Arturo DeVille, the underboss. Never the don. I turn my eyes back to Luca. "Did he call you personally?"

"Yes. He just said he wants to discuss business, no other details."

"I know they mostly deal with drugs. I heard my grandfather mention it once, but that's it. My father might know more." I look at Damian. "Did Luca meet with Ajello before?"

"Not as far as I know. And he would have mentioned something like that."

"Then it's safe to ask Francesco," Luca says. "I'll call him to let him know we're coming over for a coffee." He bends and bites my ear lightly, then whispers, "Go, change. That pink dress I like. I'm taking you with me, and we can go somewhere for lunch on our way back."

I stand up from the table and head toward the door, but then stop and look at Luca over my shoulder. "I think I'm going to wear the navy one."

"Isabella."

I smile inwardly at his tone. It riles him up no end when I decline to follow his orders. "Yes?"

"The pink dress."

"If you insist." I smile and resume walking.

I'm halfway to the dining room door when I hear Damian whisper, "You need to loosen up your reins, Luca, or she'll flip out."

I smile. If only Damian knew how much his brother's commands turn me on...

When I get inside the car with Luca twenty minutes later, wearing the pink dress, of course, he's unusually quiet, seemingly focused on his thoughts. I let it slide, but when he doesn't say a word until almost halfway to the Agostini mansion, I decide he's brooded enough.

"What is it?" I ask.

"Nothing."

"Luca," I sigh, "just spill it."

He grinds his teeth and squeezes the steering wheel. "Am I too extreme? Do you need me to 'loosen the reins,' as Damian put it?"

"Is this about the clothes thing?"

"Everything," he says and looks at me. "Do you need me to loosen the reins, Isabella?"

"No. But maybe you could reciprocate in some way." I smirk and lean to whisper in his ear. "I've been thinking, if you get to keep your finger in my pussy while I sleep, I get to do this while you drive."

Smiling, I reach my left hand over and place it on his crotch, putting a little pressure in just the right spot. The car swivels slightly while his cock hardens under my palm. Luca turns his head to look at me and his nostrils flare. I press a little harder and he inhales sharply.

"From now on," he says, "when you're driving with me, that's where your hand will be. The whole time. Am I clear Isabella?"

"Of course, Luca."

He looks at me sideways and I see a corner of his lips curve slightly. "When we get back home, I'm going to fuck you so hard, you won't be able to walk."

"I'm looking forward to it." I squeeze his cock.

Luca

"Salvatore Ajello?" Francesco's hand stills halfway to the coffee cup, his eyes wide. "Crime families rarely go into business ventures together. Too much possibility for a conflict of interest. And I've never heard of the New York Family reaching out to someone for collaboration. From what I've heard, he rarely leaves New York. And members of other families are strongly"—he clears his throat—"discouraged from visiting his region unless specifically invited."

"What if someone ventures there without invitation?" Isabella throws in.

During the drive, we agreed she'll ask the questions, so as not to raise any suspicions in the event I slip up and mention Ajello in front of Francesco at some point.

"He ends up being sent back home. In a body bag. Sometimes in more than one bag," Francesco says, then turns to me. "Be careful, Luca. That man is not to be taken lightly."

"Have you met him?" Isabella asks.

"No. But your grandfather did. He didn't like him. He

said, and I quote, 'There are ruthless people, and then there is Salvatore Ajello.' He didn't elaborate other than mentioning that he'd never met a man who seemed so dead inside."

"Sounds promising." I smile. "How old is he?"

"I have no idea. He was a capo until he took over the Family two years ago, so I assume he's in his forties or fifties. There are no photos of him that I know of. I've never heard of him visiting any public event. The way he took over the don's position created quite an uproar. He stormed into the Family meeting and killed the old don and the other six capos."

"A maniac." I snort. Perfect.

Francesco leans over the table. "If you do agree to collaborate on something with him, it could potentially make us millions. Nobody can confirm it, but rumor has it he owns half of New York."

"We'll see." I shrug and take a sip of my coffee.

Chapter Nineteen

Isabella

L UCA WALKS THROUGH THE FRONT DOOR AS I AM descending the stairs and the moment his eyes land on me, his eyebrows furrow. He passes his gaze down my white shirt and tight beige miniskirt, then moves his eyes back to lock them with mine. I smirk and lean my hip on the banister, enjoying the look of displeasure that passes his face. Without breaking eye contact, he slowly climbs the stairs and stops on the step below me.

"I thought I picked the navy dress for you today, Isabella," he says and wraps his arm around my waist, pulling me into his body. "Did I not?"

"You did." I tilt my head up and smile, "But I wanted to see what would happen if I didn't do what you said. Maybe I was looking forward to being . . . punished for my misbehavior."

The corner of Luca's lips curves up and his hand moves lower to squeeze my butt cheek.

"To the bedroom," he whispers next to my ear, then squeezes my butt cheek again. "Run."

I squeal and dash up the stairs. When I'm in the middle of the second staircase I look down and see Luca climbing them in a relaxed manner.

"It seems like you're too old to chase after me." I smile.

Luca's eyes flare. The next moment he's running up the stairs, taking two at a time. I laugh and sprint the last few steps to the landing, then turn left. I've just reached the bedroom when I feel two strong arms wrap around my waist from behind.

"I guess I'm not that old," Luca says next to my ear.

The sound of a door banging closed behind us reaches me as Luca grabs the waistband of my skirt.

"No!" I yelp, but he already has my skirt torn along the stitches at the side. Jesus!

"Now," he whispers and places a kiss at the side of my neck, "About that dress . . ."

His hand grabs my right ass cheek, and then he slaps it. The burning sensation spreads over my skin and I bite at my lower lip, as wetness pools between my legs.

"What about the dress?" I choke out, then suck in a breath as his left hand slides down my stomach and inside my panties.

"When I tell you to wear something,"—he places his finger at my core and slides it inside—"you obey, Isabella."

"And if I don't?"

"If you don't, a punishment is in order." Two more slaps. Then a kiss, on my jaw this time. "But, based on how drenched your pussy is, it seems you quite enjoy my educational methods."

"I think I do." I smile, then moan when he adds another finger.

A deep rumbling comes from behind me, followed by the sound of my panties being torn. I hear him fumbling with his belt, and then his fingers leave my pussy. Suddenly, Luca turns me around and grabs me under my thighs, lifting me up. I wrap my arms around his neck, then suck in a breath as my back gets plastered against the door.

"I can't express how much I enjoy having my cock buried in your pretty pussy, Isabella," he says and thrusts his rock-hard length inside me.

"The feeling is mutual." I moan then bury my hands in his hair, squeezing as he pounds into me.

I walk to the closet and glance at Luca over my shoulder. "So, about this dinner. Is it some special occasion?"

"Do I need a special occasion to take you to dinner?"

"I guess not. How about the white dress? The one with the gray belt?"

"You're wearing jeans tonight," Luca says.

"Oh?" That's strange. He always picks dresses.

"The tight black ones. And that silk pink blouse. No heels."

"No heels?" I turn to face him. "What kind of dinner it is with jeans and no heels?"

"It's better if you don't wear heels the first time." There's a smug smile on his lips.

"First time for what?" I take the pants out of the closet and pull them on, before reaching for the pink blouse.

"You'll see."

I shake my head, wondering what he has in mind now.

I'm just tying the blouse when I feel Luca come to stand behind me. He places his hands on my waist and starts unbuttoning my pants.

"I thought we were going to dinner."

"We are." His hand slides into my panties, his fingers stroking my clit for a few seconds before one of them slips inside of me. "You know, I've found a solution to your problem."

"Which problem?" I breathe out, then shudder when he presses on my clit with his thumb.

"Your need to have either my cock or my finger inside of you. I can't be here all the time, so I've found an alternative to make sure your pussy doesn't feel alone."

"What . . . alternative?"

He takes a black leather box from the top shelf and puts it in my hands. "Open it."

I lift the lid and look at the object resting on a velvet cushion inside. It's an elongated C-shape, with one end thicker and the other smaller, made of silicone. "What's this?"

"It's a pussy plug." He takes the object from the box. "Pull your panties and jeans down."

I place the box on a shelf and slowly follow his instructions. I'm a little skeptical because sex toys are not something I've ever been attracted to. His thumb brushes my clit a few more times, getting me wet.

"Perfect," Luca whispers in my ear, then pulls his finger out.

I moan at the loss.

"Miss my finger?"

"Yes."

"It'll get better in a second, tesoro."

He places the pussy plug between my legs, the narrower

side at the front, and the thicker side right at my entrance. He teases my opening with the tip of the bulkier end, then slides it inside me. I gasp and grab the shelf to steady myself. The object isn't as large as his cock, but it's much larger than his finger. I take deep breaths as Luca continues until the whole thing is inside me and the narrow tip is pressed to my clit. It's an odd feeling having a foreign object lodged in me this way, but not uncomfortable.

"Pull your pants up," he says. "We'll be late for dinner."

"Do you want me to remove it? Or will you do it?"

"The toy stays, tesoro."

"What? Inside?" I look at him over my shoulder in shock, but he just smiles.

When we're both dressed and ready to go, he saunters over and presses his palm over my pussy. "Looks like a perfect fit. No one will even notice it since it was specifically designed to be wearable."

The situation still has me reeling when he adds, "Let's go."

I take a first, tentative step. The silicone is soft, and the pussy plug doesn't impede my progress, but my walls do brush the sides of it with every shift. It's almost like having Luca's finger in me. The narrow end nested between my folds is touching my clit, rubbing it discreetly with each movement. Another step, then one more. The odd feeling dissipates as I walk, and by the time we reach the stairway, the strangeness is gone completely, replaced with an unexpected sense of... comfort.

"So?" Luca asks next to my ear. "Do you like it?"

"Yes."

"I knew you would."

Walking down the two sets of stairs makes me feel it

even more, enough that I have to suppress the need to sigh. When we reach the car and I carefully sit down, the sensation changes again. The thick end pushes a little deeper inside me, and the other side presses onto my clit. I expected there to be at least some irritation with me sitting down, but the shape of it seems to work perfectly with my body.

"How long?" I ask when Luca gets behind the wheel.

"What, tesoro?"

"How long do I get to . . . wear it."

He smiles. "Addicted already? I knew you would be. You're too used to having my finger inside you." He slides his palm between my legs and applies light pressure on the new toy, making me moan. "You wear it whenever I'm not in a position to keep my finger or my cock in you, Isabella. Is that clear?"

"Yes."

"I'll wake you up in the morning before I leave for work and help you place it. And I'm the only one allowed to remove it. You can do it yourself only when you need to go to the bathroom."

"Okay." I lean toward him to whisper in his ear, "You are one kinky man, Luca."

"So I am. Does it bother you?"

"Not even a little." I kiss him and slide my hand down his chest until it rests on his crotch. "I like your wickedness."

"Isabella, behave."

I smile. "Are there bigger sizes available?"

"Yes. Why?"

"This one feels like having your fingers inside of me," I say and lick his earlobe. "I'd like to have one that would make me feel like I have your cock there."

When I feel him harden under my palm, a grin spreads across my face. The fact that I can make him hard just by saying such things to him turns me on so much.

"It would feel amazing having you remove it just to replace it with your cock." I add, "I would probably come in the process."

He sucks in a breath and grabs the back of my neck. "If you continue, there won't be dinner tonight, Isabella."

"Will you?" I squeeze his cock lightly. "Get me a bigger one?"

"Yes. But you only get to wear it when I say so."

Chapter Twenty

Luca

I take a sip of my coffee, pretending to be engrossed in something on my phone while I watch my surroundings. I agreed to meet with Ajello at seven p.m., but when I proposed a restaurant downtown, he rejected the idea, picking a small family-run café in the suburbs. Strange choice, but I accepted. What's even more interesting is he insisted on taking a table outdoors. If he arrives with a convoy of bodyguards, it's bound to attract the attention of anyone passing by. Whatever. I only brought Marco, but he's waiting in the car.

Out of the corner of my eye, I spot a man crossing the street. I'm not sure what possesses me to keep my gaze focused on him because there's nothing that stands out. He appears to be in his late twenties or early thirties, has dark hair, and is wearing a black suit without a jacket. Tall. Athletic. Women would probably find him handsome, but then again, nothing overly special. The only out-of-the-ordinary thing about him is a black leather glove on his left hand. As he enters the coffee shop's patio, heading in my direction, I notice that he has a slight limp in his gait. It's very subtle, and I wouldn't have spotted it if I wasn't so focused on him. He approaches the table, takes the chair across from me, and sits down.

"Mr. Rossi." He leans back in his chair. "I'm glad to be meeting you in person, at last."

"Mr. Ajello, I presume?" I ask and look around the café trying to spot his security detail.

"I don't use bodyguards, Mr. Rossi." His lips curve upward, and there is something extremely disturbing in his smile. It's not that it seems fake. I've grown accustomed to fake smiles. That's how our society works, apparently. People smile sweetly one moment, then stab you in the back the next. This, however, seems as if he knows what a smile should look like and mimics it instead. But there's nothing behind his smile. No emotion. No scheme. It's trained. Like a dancer must learn steps to the music, this man has learned to smile for a conversation, when needed. Only the movement is that of muscles matching the beat of an imagined song. Choreographed.

"So, let's get to the point of this meeting," I say.

The waitress comes to take our order. Ajello doesn't even look at her, just waves his gloved hand, keeping his gaze on mine.

"A straightforward man. I respect that." He nods. "I've been widening my construction operations lately, a very comfortable way for laundering drug money, and I have a business proposition for you, Mr. Rossi."

"I'm listening."

"You buy and sell real estate to launder your money. It must be tiring, searching for available properties to purchase all the time. Wouldn't it be easier to have a constant supply of top-notch locations?"

"It would." I nod "Are you offering to supply?"

"Yes."

"What amount of net worth are we talking about?"

"Twenty million. Monthly."

I think about his offer. "Why me? Why not someone else?"

"You're the head of your Family. A don. You know how things work in our world, but you're also a businessman. Bogdan doesn't like you, which is a compliment in my book. He also says you drive a hard bargain."

So, he also has dealings with the Romanians. Good to know.

"I'm interested." I nod.

"Perfect. I'll send you the details." As he stands up, he places his hands on the tabletop, and I notice that the last two fingers on his gloved hand are in a slightly unnatural position, as if he can't fully extend them. "I hope we'll have a fruitful collaboration, Mr. Rossi."

I regard him as he leaves, wondering why he murdered all the other capos. If his only aim was to take over the New York Family, killing the previous don would have been enough.

Leaving money for the coffee on the table, I rise but immediately grab the side of the chair as pain slashes through my temples. It lasts for a second or two, and then it's gone. The fucking headaches are getting worse. I'll go in for that checkup as soon as I'm done with the damn banquet.

Now, I can't wait to get home, and back to my wife. I wonder if I was always this crazy about her, or if it's something that's built up after we were married and before the crash. It seems unhealthy, how I can't stop thinking about her even for a moment. Even when I'm working, Isabella is constantly on my mind. Her eyes. Her hair. The way she likes to snuggle into me every night. But most of all, it's her strong-minded personality. Her courage. She keeps amazing me every single day, this slip of a girl, who keeps playing this game, fooling the whole Family. She knew what was at stake from the beginning. I didn't. It was only a few days ago that Damian explained it to me. If anyone finds out that Isabella has been covering for me, hiding my condition, the Family will proclaim her a traitor—someone who's been acting against the Family's interests. A punishment for such an act is usually death.

If I'd known this sooner, I never would have allowed her to get tangled up in this shit. There's no coming back now. I'm not afraid of dying. But if the truth does come out at some point, and if anyone even so much as thinks about hurting Isabella, they better come at us with all they have. Because I am going to annihilate any man who tries harming a hair on my wife's head.

Chapter Twenty-one

Luca

"Lorenzo insists on seeing me tomorrow," I say as I'm unbuttoning my shirt. "I don't know why he insists. We can talk business at the banquet on Saturday."

"He wants to make himself feel important. Low self-esteem complex," Isabella says from the bed. "Especially now, with you as the head of the Family."

"Do you want to come? He's booked us a table at Mirage."

"Of course, he has," she snorts. Getting off the bed, she stands behind me and wraps her arms around my waist. "He knows you'll be paying the bill. Is it okay if I come? It's a business meeting after all."

"I don't give a fuck that it is." I take the box I picked up this morning from the specialty shop I've started visiting frequently and place it on a dresser. "I've bought you something."

"What?" She peeks around me, and I see her eyes widen upon seeing the leather box. "Is it . . . ?"

"Yes." I take her arm and pull her around to stand in front of me. "Want to try it on?"

"Is it much bigger?" she asks and reaches for the box, but I catch her hand in mine.

"It's bigger. Close your eyes."

She shuts her eyes immediately, and I smile. Who would've expected someone as young as her to be so eager and responsive to all my unconventional ways. Moving my palms down her generous hips, I slide her panties down and wrap my fingers around the object lodged in her pussy. Two days ago, I decided to punish her for not putting on the dress I requested and removed her pussy plug. She whimpered and begged me to put it back, pressing her small hands over her pussy the whole time. I buried my cock inside of her instead. My little addict. Isabella can't bear the thought of not having my cock or something else that reminds her of me inside her. Her reactions make me so hard that it feels like I'm going to explode.

As expected, she starts complaining the moment I take out the toy, so I temporarily push my finger inside her. "Keep your eyes closed," I say and open the box.

I take the new pussy plug from the box. I've already washed it and put a good amount of lubricant over the thick end because it's significantly larger than the one she's accustomed to.

"Spread your legs slightly. Yes, just like that." I place the tip of the new pussy plug at her entrance, pull out my finger and start sliding the sleek black toy inside her pussy.

"Everything okay?" I ask when her breathing hitches. "If it's too much, I'll stop."

"Don't stop." She breathes out and squeezes my wrist. "I want it all in. Now, Luca."

I slide it fully inside, then adjust the thinner tip so it presses on her clit. "Good?"

"What if it slides out?" she asks.

"It won't, tesoro." I press my palm over her pussy. "Let's try walking, hmm?"

She steps forward and I follow without taking my hand off her. "See? It won't slide out. You just need to get accustomed to a bigger size. Let's try a few more steps."

When she starts walking toward the bed, I let go of her pussy. "How does it feel?"

She turns to face me and lowers herself to the bed. Her movements are slow, her eyes closed as if she's savoring the feeling. When she's seated and moans, I can barely restrain myself from grabbing and fucking her senseless.

"How does it feel?" she repeats my question, biting her lower lip, and opens her eyes. "It feels like I have your cock inside of me, Luca."

"You need to be really wet to use this one, Isabella. If you're not, use lubricant. If you hurt yourself, I'll throw it away. You hear me?"

"Yes."

I take her chin, tilt her head up, and trace her bottom lip with my thumb. "Now, let's remove it."

"No."

"Yes, Isabella. When I'm around, you get my cock," I say and start unbuttoning my pants. "On the bed, please."

I lower myself over her and reach to pull out the pussy plug. With the toy gone, I slide my cock inside her heat. Isabella pants and moans as I bury myself in her.

Instead of pounding into her hard, I slowly slide out, then in again, watching her face the whole time, enjoying the sounds of pleasure that leave her lips. My young little wife whom I've corrupted with my wicked ways. I don't know what I felt for her before, but I know what I feel now, hearing her moan my name. I thrust into her again, and she starts shaking under me, but I keep sliding in and out, letting her ride the orgasm, and only allow myself to come after she's done. When her body goes limp beneath me, I bend my head to whisper next to her ear, "I am so fucking in love with you, Isabella." Then, I crash my lips to hers.

Isabella

I watch him as he sleeps, his thick eyebrows, mouth that does the most sinful things, hair falling freely over his face. *My Luca.* I lean into him, tucking my face into his neck and inhaling his scent.

He told me he loves me last night. I never dared to hope those words would fall from his lips. It was always an impossible dream. And now that I've finally heard the words I've been so desperate for, instead of being overjoyed, I'm scared shitless. What if his memory comes back? I don't think I could take it if Luca goes back to being his old self. It would be even worse than before the accident if he knows I tricked him into believing the farce I've created.

An arm wraps around my midsection, and suddenly I'm facing the wall with my back pressed to Luca's chest.

"What did I tell you? How do you sleep?" he asks, his words whispered in my ear.

"With your finger in me," I say as his finger circles my clit and then slips inside, making me gasp.

"If I ever again catch you lying next to me in any other way, there will be consequences, Isabella."

"What kind of consequences?"

"I'm going to keep you in bed"—his finger slides out then in again—"the whole fucking day,"—he pinches my clit—"torturing you like this, without letting you come."

His finger vanishes from my core, and I cry out, grabbing his hand and pressing it over my pussy. "Please, Luca."

"Please, what? What do you need?"

"Your cock. Inside me." I squeeze my legs together, trying to relieve myself of at least some of the yearning in my core.

He turns me, his big hands holding on to my waist, and positions me above his cock, its tip teasing my entrance. I try sinking onto it, but he keeps me clutched in his grip, denying me the gratification.

"Do we have an understanding, Isabella? About the sleeping arrangement?"

"Yes." I nod, gripping his forearms. "Please. I can't take it anymore."

"Is this better?" he asks as he lowers me onto his cock.

I breathe deeply, marveling at the feel of him filling me up so completely. I start rotating my hips, trying to take even more of him inside. Luca's hand comes to rest where our bodies are joined, and he massages my clit as he pumps into me from below. I'm already close when his hands come under my ass, and he lifts me only to slam me down onto his cock again. A scream escapes me as I feel the orgasm nearing. I close my eyes. He raises my body again, and I arch my back when his length invades my pussy in the next moment. Up. Down. Up. Down. The pressure in my core skyrockets, and I come with another scream.

When I slump onto his chest, his cock still feels hard, and his breathing is labored. I tilt my head up and raise my eyebrows at him. "Why didn't you finish?"

"I like the feel of my cock inside you too much," he says through gritted teeth.

"Luca . . ." I reach out and place my hand on his cheek, trying not to laugh. "You'll give yourself a heart attack from the strain, baby."

"No!" he barks. "And don't you dare move. I'm holding on by a thread."

"And how long do you plan on us staying like this?"

"For as long as I can control myself. Don't fucking move, Isabella."

He's crazy. I won't let him do this to himself.

"I need to tell you something," I say.

"What?"

"When I went to the hairdressers yesterday, I removed the pussy plug."

His eyes widen and his hands squeeze my ass cheeks. "You did what?" he growls. "For how long?"

"Two hours."

His breathing quickens, and he stares at me, his nostrils flaring. "You left the house with nothing to remind you how my cock feels?"

"Yes."

I didn't, actually. I planned to. I wanted to see if I could manage without it for so long, but I only got to the car before the need became too much, and I rushed back to the bedroom. If someone told me previously that I'd be using sex toys, especially in such an extreme way, I would've thought they were nuts.

The vein on his neck starts pulsing. Wrapping his arm around my middle, he rolls us until I'm on my back, then gathers my wrists with his hand pinning them above my head.

"You,"—he slams into me—"will never,"—another thrust—"fucking ever..."

I moan as my pussy starts spasming around his cock again. It should have been too soon, but seeing Luca losing it like this, turns me on beyond measure.

"...leave the house without it." Another thrust. "Do you understand, Isabella?"

"Yes, Luca."

He groans as his orgasm hits when the words leave my lips, and I shatter.

Chapter Twenty-Two

Luca

"Turn right here," Isabella says when we reach the intersection. "It's there, just next to the big flower shop."

I follow her directions and park in front of the building with a glass façade. Even from the outside, it's visible that the restaurant is high-end kind of place. Each car parked in the lot is priced at more than a hundred grand. I can't see the inside because the glass is mirrored, but I know it has black wood finishings and tall ceilings with fancy iron chandeliers. In the center, there's a huge round space with an open ceiling where the best tables are set. I know all that without having any recollection of ever visiting the place. I've been here. Before.

It's taken me some time to accept the concept of *before*. The first few days after the crash, I was sure my memory would come back. Every time I woke up, I expected the recollections to hit me, certain that my loss was temporary. When Isabella and Damian started filling me in on the details of my life, I assumed that some of it would trigger my brain and start an avalanche of memories. It didn't. Neither did coming home. Facing my daughter was my last chance for something to spark my memories. There was no spark, however. No trigger of any kind. I saw the girl with long black hair running into my arms, and I felt not even an inkling of recognition. The moment I held Rosa in my embrace, I decided I would accept the situation as it was. I stopped dwelling on the possibility of my memory and old life returning someday. In a way, I decided to cut my losses and focus on the now. The *before* became only a time marker.

"Have I brought you here at some point?" I ask as I help Isabella out of the car. She's wearing a navy silk dress that's adorned with lace and flows over her upper body and flares out from the waist. I've chosen it for her. I keep picking dresses that have flowy skirts because the idea of another man ogling her ass makes me go ballistic. Her pretty behind is only mine to look at.

"Nope." She shrugs. "I came here once with Angelo."

"Angelo Scardoni?"

"Yes. We were kind of engaged."

I grab her hand and turn her to face me. "What?"

"It was just an agreement that my father set up when I was eighteen. Nothing came out of it, as you already know," she says and smiles. "But I have to say, you are sexy when you're jealous."

"So why did he take you to dinner?"

"Because I wanted to go out with someone, hoping it would cure me of my crush on you, Luca." She raises her free hand and takes my chin between her fingers. "A hint for you. It didn't. Nothing and no one managed to make me even slightly interested in anyone other than you."

"He's ten years younger than me," I say through my teeth.

"But he isn't you. I've always wanted you." She squeezes my chin. "You. No one else."

I stare at her, then grab her around the waist and bring her flush with my chest. Then, I slam my mouth to hers.

Isabella

I know we're fucked the moment we step inside the restaurant and my eyes find the table at the center where Lorenzo is sitting. He's not alone. Sitting next to him is a man in his midthirties, with sandy blond hair and glasses. He stands up when he sees us approaching, a wide smile on his face. Davide Barbini. Lorenzo's nephew. And one of Luca's friends from school.

My heart explodes into an insane tempo while my brain works in overdrive as I try, and fail, to come up with a way to get us out of this shitstorm. Damian and I never briefed Luca on his childhood friends because none of them had anything to do with Cosa Nostra. None, except Davide Barbini, who moved to Italy two years ago and should have stayed there, damn it!

There's no time to warn Luca because we've nearly reached their table. They'd notice if I tried to say something to him. And we can't just turn around and leave. Fuck! Think!

A fifteen-step distance divides us from our demise, and I have nothing. There's no way Luca can pull off a whole meal without slipping. Ten steps. There will be high school jokes and mentions of other friends from that time. We're doomed.

Six steps. The sound of high-pitched laughter reaches me

from our right. My head snaps to the side, my eyes finding a blonde woman sitting at the table in the corner, laughing at something one of her friends said. Simona. I never would have thought that seeing Luca's ex would make me so happy. I could kiss that bitch right now. Two steps. Lorenzo rises from his chair. It's now or never.

I pull my hand out of Luca's, turn toward him abruptly, and start yelling into his face. "How could you!"

Luca

I stare at Isabella, stunned. What the fuck?

"You did it on purpose, didn't you?" she continues. "Asking me to accompany you, when you knew she would be here!"

Everyone at the restaurant, including Lorenzo and the blond man with him, have gone deadly quiet. I have no idea who the guy is.

"Isabella, calm down," I say, reaching for her hand. I don't know what's riled her up so much to make a scene with at least sixty people watching.

"Calm down?" she shouts, pointing with her finger to her left. "I know you've been cheating on me with your ex, but to insist we come to the same restaurant where you knew she'd be?"

"What?" I look to the table she's pointing at and see Simona sitting there, looking as shocked as everyone else.

"I let the incident with the maid go," Isabella keeps

shouting, waving her hands through the air. "But this... this is too much! I'm not staying here a second more."

An incident with a maid? What the fuck is she talking about? We both know it's utter nonsense. Something's going on here. From what I know about Isabella—and I think I know her very well by now—she'd never make a fool of herself in front of an audience. Not without a reason.

"Isabella," I say and try to place my arm around her, but she moves away a step.

"Fuck you, Luca," she sneers at me and storms toward the exit.

I watch her leave, then turn toward Lorenzo and the blond guy. They too are staring at the door Isabella just went through.

"Looks like you have a problem, Luca." The blond guy laughs and looks directly at me just as a jolt of pain pierces my brain. I don't worry about the fact that he knows who I am. Instead, I turn my back to them and head for the exit.

"We'll talk tomorrow, Lorenzo," I call over my shoulder and leave the restaurant, stalking after my exhibitionist wife.

I find Isabella standing next to our car, leaning on the door with her eyes closed. Another pang hits me as I walk toward her. When I reach her, I place my hands on either side of her, caging her in against the car.

"You made a fool out of yourself there, tesoro." I bend until our faces are at the same level.

"I know," she says, keeping her eyes closed. "And with Simona there to witness it, I'm sure the whole Cosa Nostra will know what happened within an hour."

"It was because of that guy who was with Lorenzo, wasn't it?"

"Davide Barbini." She nods. "You two went to school together. If we'd have stayed, it would've been a disaster. We needed an out."

"So, you made a fool of yourself because of me?" I lift my hand and place it at the back of her neck.

Isabella's eyes open and she looks at me, holding my gaze. "There are not many things that I wouldn't do for you, Luca. You should know that already."

I watch her for a few moments, etching her defiant eyes and stubborn chin on my very being it seems, then I crash my mouth against her lips in a soul-shuttering kiss.

Chapter Twenty-Three

Luca

It happens suddenly as I'm buttoning my shirt the morning of the banquet.

Isabella's in the bathroom, taking a shower. I woke her up early by sliding my cock into her while she was still asleep. With all the people arriving to make preparations for tonight, she'll be busy the whole day, and there won't be any time for us until late into the night. There's no way I could let her go the entire day without having my cock inside her.

It starts with another sharp pang, but this time the pain doesn't dissipate right away. Instead, it keeps slashing across my temples in waves so strong I have to sit down on the bed. I squeeze my eyes closed, waiting for it to pass, but the pain keeps building until I feel like my head is going to explode. Then, as suddenly as it started, the pain is gone. I should feel relief, but I can't move from my spot on the bed while I'm trying to sort out the chaos raging in my brain.

When I allowed myself to consider the possibility of re-
gaining my memory, I always assumed it will be a gradua

process—remembering one person at a time, or certain events, randomly. I never expected it to hit me like a sledgehammer, but that's how it feels. One moment all I know is the last two months of my life, and the next, the past thirty-five years materialize out of nowhere.

The bathroom door opens, and Isabella rushes out, clutching her phone to her ear while she's adjusting her dress. "Let them in, I'll be right down," she says into the phone, then looks at me. "The decoration company is early, I have to go."

"All right." I nod, staring at her.

"Are you going to the office?"

"Yes."

"Don't be late for your own party." She points the phone in my direction. "If I finish up early, I might drop by your office around noon."

I get up and walk across the room. When I'm standing before her, I take her face in my palms and just stare at her.

"Luca? Is something wrong?"

"No," I say, not breaking our locked gazes. "Why?"

"You have a very strange look in your eyes."

The phone in her hand rings again. Isabella sighs, then tilts her head up to press her lips to mine. "I really have to go," she says into my mouth.

I follow her with my eyes as she hurries out of the room—my extraordinarily brilliant wife, whom I so wrongly accused of being too young to deal with me and my line of work. Two months. For two fucking months she guided me about while I didn't have a damn clue who all the people around me were. She managed to trick the whole damn Family into believing there was nothing wrong with her husband. Or, it seems, everyone except one person.

I grab my jacket off the chair, take the car keys and my wallet, and head for the door. Tonight's banquet is bound to be much more interesting than I imagined because, along with my life, I also remember the face of the man who tried to kill me, and he'll probably be here.

Yes, it will be a very exciting evening.

There's a knock at the office door, and Isabella's head peeks inside. "Am I interrupting?"

"I'll call you later, Franco," I say into the phone and motion for her to come in.

She walks to my desk, removes her sunglasses, and places them and her purse on the wooden surface. I study her, focusing on how her gray dress dips into her cleavage, leaving nothing to the imagination.

"I don't remember approving that outfit for today."

"Because you haven't." She stands before me, bends, and starts unbuttoning my pants. "So, I came to make amends."

My cock instantly gets hard. "All right. I'll allow it this time. But you won't do it again. Is that clear?"

"Yes, Luca."

My cock swells even more. It's unbelievable how much it turns me on when she's obedient because I know there isn't a single submissive bone in her body. Isabella is not a woman who'd ever let a man control her in any way, yet, she's compliant with my orders. What's even a greater turn-on is knowing that she likes it.

"You may proceed." I lean back in my chair.

Isabella kneels between my legs, takes out my cock and

brings her lips to the tip. She licks it, then takes it into her mouth and starts sucking. I grip the sides of the chair, trying to restrain myself from coming into her mouth right away.

"Are you wearing your pussy plug, Isabella?"

She gives my cock one slow lick, then looks up and smiles. "No."

"Why?"

"I came here intending to get something better inside of me." She slides her hand down my length and squeezes it lightly. "I left my panties at home, as well."

I growl, then bend to grab around her waist and hoist her onto my lap, right over my rock-hard dick. She moans as I slide into her, wriggling her hips and taking all of me.

I paw her ass, lift and slowly slide her back down as she moans and grabs my shoulders. The feel of Isabella on my lap, with my cock lodged inside her, is priceless. Unfortunately, the position doesn't allow much space for maneuvering. I swipe my right hand over my desk, pushing the folders and other stuff off the top.

"Luca!" Isabella yelps, looking down at the papers littering the floor.

Holding under her thighs, I get up off the chair and deposit her sweet ass on my desk. The laptop is lying open right behind her back. She may hurt herself if she leans back, so I grab the thing and send it to the floor, as well.

"Are you out of your fucking mind?" She stares at me.

"On the contrary, tesoro." I cup her butt cheeks in my palms and pull her toward the edge of the desk. "Lock your legs behind me and hold on."

The moment she obeys, I thrust myself back inside of her. It feels so fucking good when her walls clutch at my cock while she watches me with those magnificent eyes. I'm not sure what I love more—Isabella's breathtakingly sinful body, her unrelenting and steely spirit, or her brilliant mind. I'm crazy about everything where my young wife is concerned.

A mewl leaves her lips when I start pounding into her, and I soak up every single sound as I demolish her. When I feel her walls trembling around my cock, I stop holding myself back and let go, filling her up with my cum.

My desk phone rings. It somehow escaped the same fate that befell the laptop and the folders. I maintain my hold on Isabella as I sit back down on the chair, then reach for the phone.

"Donato, I'm busy," I answer the phone.

Isabella starts to move, trying to stand up, but I squeeze my arm around her to keep her flush to my body. I like the feel of my cock inside of her.

"There's a problem with the newest arms delivery," Donato says. "We're two crates of grenades short."

There's a lick at the side of my neck. Then, on my jaw, a bite.

"Deduct the amount equal to the cost of six crates, and wire Bogdan the money."

Hands in my hair. A kiss at the corner of my mouth.

"Six?" Donato gulps. "What if he raises an issue?"

I turn my head and our gazes meet. She smiles mischievously and presses her lips to mine.

"Just remind him of the last discussion he and I had," I say into Isabella's lips, throw the phone on my desk, and wrap my hand around her throat.

"What are you wearing tonight?" I ask, sliding my hand up to cup her jaw.

"No restrictions?" She arches her eyebrows.

"No restrictions." I press my lips to hers. "But only for tonight."

She smiles, wraps her arms around my neck, and removes my hair tie. "You were right, you know? I *am* obsessed with your hair," she says and tunnels her fingers through the strands. "My first memory of you is like this. It was wet then, though."

"I know, Isa."

Isabella's fingers go still. Fuck. I never meant that to slip out. I planned on telling her tonight that I remember everything.

"Damian told me I saved you, pulled you out of the pool when you were six," I add.

"You did." She smiles. "I should head back. There are still some last-minute checks to be made, and I have to change."

"Make sure it's not something too revealing, or I may change my mind."

Her lips widen more. "What if it is?"

I tilt her head sideways to whisper in her ear, "There will be consequences, Isabella. You know that."

"Yes."

"Good." I lean forward and press the intercom button on my desk phone. "Magda, bring me today's listings."

"Right away, Mr. Rossi."

Isabella shifts, intending to get off my lap, but I tighten my arm around her, keeping her in place.

"Luca? Your secretary will be here any second."

"I know." I kiss her shoulder, grab her butt cheeks and reposition her on my, once again, hard cock. "And you're staying right where you are. Is that clear, Isabella?"

She's silent for a few moments, then turns her head so her lips are just near my ear. "Yes, Mr. Rossi," she whispers, and my cock hardens even more.

"Do you have any idea"—she starts moving her pelvis forward, then back, slowly—"how much it turns me on"—a slight rotation of her hips—"when you order me around?"

I grit my teeth, trying to stay composed, but a growl still manages to leave my lips. "Tell me."

"It makes me so wet that I'm seriously considering wearing two pairs of panties if you continue." She bites my earlobe. "You know what makes me even wetter?"

Jesus. Don't say it.

"When I obey, Luca."

I explode inside of her the instant my name leaves her lips. "Fuck."

There's a knock at the door, and Magda enters holding a stack of papers in her hand but then stops midstep. Her gaze passes over the overturned laptop on the floor, the papers scattered about, and finally stops on Isabella sitting on my lap. The desk provides some cover, but she can't have missed Isabella's dress pulled up to just below her breasts.

"I-i-is it a bad time?" she stutters.

Isabella straightens on my lap and throws a look over her shoulder. "Not at all, Magda. Please leave the papers on the sofa."

My secretary rushes to drop off the papers, then hightails it out of the office in record time, closing the door with a bang.

"I need two minutes," I say through my teeth. I can't believe I came without waiting for her. Like I'm some teenager.

"No time. I have to go back home."

I squeeze her ass. "You're not leaving this office with a lower orgasm score than me."

Holding her under her ass, I stand up and carry her to the bathroom, where I clean us up, then carry her back. I set her onto the desk, sit down in my chair, and place my hands behind her knees. "Lie down."

"What if someone comes in?"

"They'll turn around and leave." I fix her with my gaze. "Down. Spread your legs."

"If you say so, Mr. Rossi." She smiles and lowers her back onto the desk.

Isabella

I fasten the last button at the back of my neck and look at myself in the mirror. The beige material of the dress hugs my body from the high neckline to slightly below the knees, emphasizing my curves. I turn and look at myself from the side, and then from the back, focusing on my hips. The shapewear that I put on under the dress works wonders. My butt seems at least two sizes smaller. Maybe even three.

When I first got dressed for tonight, I regretted the fact I let Luca convince me to gain back the weight I'd previously lost. I kind of got carried away and instead of putting on only those ten pounds, I packed on fifteen more. It wasn't that hard, I just stopped counting calories as rigorously as I usually do. I wish I didn't. The most hilarious thing is that I'm still wearing the same size shirts. All that extra weight, and my breasts became only slightly fuller. Everything else ended up in the bottom part of my body—some on my thighs, but mostly my hips and ass. Just like I feared it would.

I wasn't insecure about my body until the moment I saw myself in the mirror, wearing this dress. My eyes zeroed in on my behind, making me think of a patient whose butt implant surgery had gone terribly wrong. I almost took off the dress, initially, thinking I'd put on something less tight. But then I remembered the crazy body-shaping underwear I bought on a whim. It's really tight and rather uncomfortable, but I don't care. Maybe I should start wearing it every day, at least until I manage to lose a few inches around my hips.

It's genetics. My mother has a similar pear-shaped build—narrow upper body and significant behind. Grandma was the same. But I seemed to have ended up with the most well-endowed . . . back end. Thank God Luca usually wants me to wear dresses. That allows me to hide the size my butt has reached. I doubt he's noticed it when we're intimate. Men don't usually notice that kind of thing during sex.

The image of Simona comes to my mind. She's much taller than me, but I don't think that, even at fifteen, I would have been able to get into her current size pants. Luca keeps saying he likes my body, and I don't think he's lying, but still . . . He must have been attracted to his ex-wife if he chose to be with her. If he was attracted to her body, how can he like mine, which is the total opposite?

Enough. Now is not the time for insecurities when there are close to fifty people arriving shortly and expecting everything to be perfect. Maybe I should check the guest list one more time, just to make sure I didn't miss anyone I should brief Luca on. I comb my hand through my hair, which I've left down, check my reflection in the mirror one last time to make sure the lines of the shapewear are not visible, and leave the bathroom.

Luca is sitting in the recliner at the opposite side of the room, typing on his phone. When I enter, he lifts his head, checking me out.

"You're the most beautiful thing I've ever set my eyes on," he says with a satisfied smile on his lips, then moves his gaze lower, but he stops midway. "Turn around."

I raise my eyebrows but make a slow turn. As my eyes return to him, he isn't smiling anymore.

"Are you on a diet again, Isabella?"

"No. Why?"

"Your ass is smaller."

So, he's noticed. "I'm wearing shapewear underneath the dress," I say. "Do you like it?"

"Shapewear?" He scowls. "What the fuck is that?"

"It's worn underneath clothes to make the body look slimmer." I pass my palms down my legs one more time, checking for the visible seams. "It's damn tight but it works great."

Luca's nostrils flare and his eyes narrow. "Remove that crap."

"What?"

"Now, Isabella."

I grit my teeth, pull the dress up to my waist and take off the slimming shorts I had on underneath. Throwing them away, I straighten my dress again.

"There. Satisfied?" I snap. He doesn't say anything, just watches me. Maybe he doesn't like the idea of shapewear. "I only planned on wearing it until I got back to my old weight, okay?"

Luca still doesn't say a word. The stretchy material of

the dress clings to my body, showing every extra pound I've gained. I wait for him to tell me to put the shaping shorts on again when he suddenly stands up from the recliner and, leaving the phone, stalks toward me. Is he mad at me? He can't be mad because I've gained weight, can he? The expression on his face is really strange. I take a step back, then a few more until I end up in the bathroom again, with Luca following me inside. He bends his head, his breath brushing my cheek as his hands come to his belt, and he starts unclasping it. I watch with wide eyes as he unbuttons his pants and releases his cock that's already fully erect.

"Turn around," he says.

I turn my back to him, slightly confused, and feel his hands land on my ass.

"Jesus." He sucks in a breath. "I could come just from looking at you."

"You . . . like it?"

"Oh, tesoro." He grabs my hips and presses me against his body. "Why did you put that slimming crap on?"

"I . . . my ass is enormous, and this dress is really tight. It shows everything. I thought you wouldn't find it attractive."

"Hmm. Want me to demonstrate to you what I think about your body?" He bends his head to whisper into my ear, "Just to make sure there are no misunderstandings?"

"Okay?"

"Take a step forward so I can see you better." He moves his hands from my butt cheeks to my hips. "Perk your ass slightly."

When I do as he says, he takes a deep breath. "Fucking perfection."

His hands leave my hips, and I hear a groan behind me. I

look up into the mirror and lock eyes with him. His right arm is moving furiously and I realize that he's jerking himself off to the sight of my ass. He screws his face up, as if he's in pain, but then a pure euphoric look comes over him as he comes. I turn around to find Luca holding his cock in his hand, cum all over his fingers. He reaches for one of the towels, cleans himself, and buttons up his pants.

"Does me coming just from looking at your ass clear things for you, tesoro?"

I nod, slightly shocked.

"Good. Are you wearing your pussy plug?" he slides his hand under my dress and presses his palm onto my panties, cupping my pussy.

"You know I am."

"Perfect. Then let's go downstairs."

Chapter Twenty-four

Luca

Isabella takes a glass from the waiter and leans toward me.

"Emiliano Caruso," she mumbles. "Damian said you two worked together on some project in January, but he doesn't have any details. Emiliano has been trying to climb the hierarchy ladder for years. He wants Donato's spot, but my grandfather wouldn't let him have it. He was the main suspect in a case involving illegal dog fights a few years back, and Nonno didn't want anyone who'd ever been on the police radar."

I nod, brush my hand down Isabella's back and place a kiss on the top of her head. We've been mingling for almost two hours. She's been giving me details on every guest as they've arrived, and I've let her, even though it's not necessary anymore. I'm not quite sure why I didn't tell her this morning that my memory has come back. Maybe because I wanted to see her in action tonight. It's amazing how much information she keeps in her brain. Over the past two days, she's filled me in on every member of the Family expected to attend the banquet, their roles, family members, and dirty laundry. People would be shocked if they were aware how many details of their lives were stored in Isabella's pretty head.

"Why did you send Rosa to her friend's house for tonight?" Isabella asks. "She was so excited about the party, especially the cake."

"I didn't want her here in case something bad happens," I say.

"It's a party, Luca. We have a ton of security. Nothing bad is going to happen."

I look down at her and brush my thumb along the line of her chin while my lips curve into a smile. "We'll see."

Isabella's eyes widen. "What are you not telling me?"

Several excited shouts come from the other side of the room, and we both look toward the commotion near the door.

"Shit!" Isabella grabs my hand and squeezes it. "What the fuck is Davide Barbini doing here? He wasn't on the guest list, and I strictly forbade the guys at the door to admit anyone who's not on it."

"It looks like Lorenzo brought him in," I say and watch my underboss standing next to his nephew while the people gather around to chat with the newcomer.

"I still don't understand what the hell Davide is doing in Chicago," she whispers.

"Yes, quite interesting, don't you think?" I smile and take her hand in mine. "Let's go say hi."

"What!" she whisper-yells. "Damian was only able to share some general info on him. What if he mentions something that happened when the two of you went to school?"

"I'll improvise."

"You'll improvise?" she snaps. "Are you crazy?"

I stop, turn her toward me and lift her chin with my finger. "Trust me, tesoro," I say and place a kiss on her lips.

The group with Lorenzo and Davide has moved to the center of the room, where more than a dozen round tables have been set. As we walk in their direction, I cast a glance at the corner where Marco is standing, and when our gazes connect, I give him a discreet nod. He tilts his head, speaking into his headpiece, and in my peripheral vision, Emilio locks the front door and blocks it with his body.

By the time we reach the center of the room, two of my security guys are positioned at each exit point. Just as I instructed. It might be overkill since this is a no-weapons-allowed event, but I don't want to risk it.

"Davide," I say and clasp him on the back. "I'm so sorry we didn't get the opportunity to catch up the other day. Let's eat and you can tell us about your life in Italy."

He opens his mouth to say something, but I push onto his shoulder until he sits down on the chair.

"You can join us, Lorenzo." I turn toward my underboss. "If I remember well, you said you have something important to discuss."

Lorenzo smiles and takes a seat next to Davide. The quick calculated look the two of them exchange doesn't escape my notice. Isabella doesn't say a word, just keeps squeezing my hand and doesn't release it even when we walk around the table and take our seats opposite them.

"I hear you had an accident two months back," Davide says. "I hope it wasn't anything serious."

"Not at all. A mild concussion. Some burns and scratches."

"You were always thick-headed, Luca." He smirks.

"Remember that time when we stole your father's car and headed to Luigi's? When we crashed not even a mile after we left the grounds?"

Isabella's hand squeezes mine under the table and I can feel her fingers are trembling. I recline in my chair and cock my head, regarding Davide, then turn my gaze to Lorenzo. He's looking at me with an evil glint in his eyes and a barely visible self-satisfied smile on his lips. Yes, it looks like I was right in my assumptions.

"You don't remember?" Davide continues, but I keep watching Lorenzo, whose smile is getting wider by the second.

Isabella

We are so fucked.

I keep my eyes glued to the table in front of me, trying to think of a way to get us out of this fuckup. Why doesn't he just say he remembers and be done with it? I can then try changing the direction of the conversation afterward.

"I can't say I remember that, Davide," Luca says next to me, and my head snaps up.

Why did he confess that? I turn my gaze on Lorenzo and find him smiling. He doesn't look surprised by Luca's answer. In fact, he seems . . . excited. The realization sets in, and I squeeze Luca's hand with all my might. How the fuck did Lorenzo find out about Luca's memory loss?

"How can you not remember?" Davide presses.

"Because it never happened, Davide," Luca says in a cold voice.

My body goes rigid. How would he know that? Did Damian tell him about that event?

"That's the story Philip told us while we were playing cards at his place." Luca continues. "It was the summer after freshman year, as I recall. Good old days."

I feel this strange falling sensation, and I'm spiraling as panic settles inside me. Oh my God, he remembers.

I don't dare look at Luca, I can't bear to see the loathing on his face. He probably hates me now. It's over. Squeezing my lips together, I rein in the tears that threaten to fall and try pulling my hand out of Luca's grasp. The grip he has around my fingers only gets stronger. Taking a deep breath, I somehow gather the courage to look up at him, but instead of a look of anger which I expected to find, I see a smug smile pulling at his lips. His hand lifts to my face, and he brushes away a stray tear with his thumb. My eyes widen as he leans forward to place a quick kiss on my lips, then turns to Davide.

"I wonder, Davide," he says, "what were you promised in exchange for running me off that road?"

With his face turned ghostly white, Davide stares at Luca. A chair screeches, and in the next moment, Davide launches toward the nearest door. Marco catches him halfway there.

The room has gone silent.

"Boss." Marco turns to Luca. "Where should we put him?"

"Kitchen will do," Luca says. "We have a tiled floor there, it's easier to wash away the blood."

Marco nods and starts dragging Davide toward the door on the opposite side of the room. Most of the guests were in the middle of their meals, but now, everyone has stopped eating, and dozens of eyes are staring at Davide, who thrashes

RUINED SECRETS

and yells as he tries to free himself. Marco backhands him, then keeps hauling him in the direction of the kitchen.

The door on the left suddenly flies opens and three men walk in, followed by Emilio and Tony. I don't recognize the first two, but the one that follows is one of Lorenzo's bodyguards. Their hands are tied behind their backs, and they have bruises all over their faces. Emilio nudges one of them with his gun, and the guy stumbles. I shift my gaze to Lorenzo, who's sitting rigidly in his chair, staring at the tied men.

"To the kitchen, as well. I'll take care of them later." Luca crosses his arms over his chest and turns to Lorenzo. "I wonder, what did you promise Davide? A capo's position when you take over the Family after I'm out of the picture? Was that the plan?"

"I have no idea what you're talking about," Lorenzo mumbles.

"No?" Luca smiles and leans into Lorenzo's face. "There was one thing that kept bugging me. Why haven't you tried again? And then it came to me. You knew I didn't remember anything. Tell me, what gave me away?"

Lorenzo watches him for a couple of seconds, then grits his teeth. "I found the doctor who treated you when you were admitted to the hospital."

"But you needed to be sure, didn't you? Before you revealed it to the Family. So, you brought Davide with you to the lunch yesterday to see how I'd react. And when that failed, you brought him here. I'm so sorry for ruining your plan."

"You took my place!" Lorenzo sneers. "It was mine! I spent decades licking Giuseppe's ass, and then you barged in, married this cunt, and fucked up everything!"

Someone gasps at a table nearby, but other than that, the room remains eerily silent.

Luca leaps from the chair, grabs Lorenzo's hair and smashes his face on the tabletop. The plates and silverware clatter from the force of the blow. Lorenzo flails, reaches for Luca's hand and tries to wriggle free, but Luca just slams his face into the table again. And again. The tableware clinks and rattles each time. Two of the plates and several glasses end up falling to the floor, the shattering of china and crystal adding to the symphony of brutality.

The gasps and murmurs among the guests continue while my husband does his best to beat the living shit out of Barbini. Eventually, Luca pulls Lorenzo up, still holding him by the hair. "Apologize to my wife."

I lean back in my chair, staring at the bloody mess of Lorenzo's face. He looks up, then spits in my general direction, bloodied spittle soiling the white tablecloth.

The eyes of the people in the room dart between Luca and Lorenzo, waiting for what will happen next.

"You know, I'm okay with you trying to kill me," Luca says, and he looks down at the table. "That's business. You tried. Failed. I shoot you in the head, and we all go back to our merry lives." He reaches for a corkscrew on the table, then steps closer to Lorenzo.

"But no one disrespects my wife, Lorenzo," Luca barks, then looks up at Marco and Emilio who are standing behind the underboss. "Hold him down."

Luca's men grip Lorenzo, keeping him in the chair. As I watch, my husband plunges the corkscrew into the side of Lorenzo's neck, just under the ear. Lorenzo screams and tries to get up off the chair, but Marco and Emilio push him back down and keep a hold of him as Luca rips the corkscrew out. Blood sprays from the wound, soaking the front of Luca's shirt, as well as Marco's hands. Several of the guests shriek.

"Did I hear an apology?" Luca bends his head as if to hear what Lorenzo is saying, but the only sounds that leave Barbini's mouth are choking noises. "Nope, I don't think it was an apology," he says and thrusts the corkscrew into Lorenzo's neck again, from the front this time.

I shut my eyes, not able to watch the bloodbath anymore. But I can't shut out the whimpering. The choking sounds. I swallow bile.

A minute or so later, the choking sounds cease, and I will myself to open my eyes. Luca is standing in front of Lorenzo, corkscrew in hand. His right arm is covered in blood. His front, too. I move my gaze to Lorenzo, or really his body, and gasp. There's a long red line around his neck, blood pouring from at least a dozen puncture wounds and flowing down his torso. Bile gathers in my throat from seeing all the blood. Grinding my teeth together, I take a deep breath and force myself to remain still. I am not fainting with the whole Family watching.

Luca turns around, pins me with his gaze and throws the bloody corkscrew on the table. I follow him with my eyes as he covers the distance between us in a few long steps and stands before me while everyone stares at him.

"I'm sorry for ruining your party, tesoro."

I blink at him. Should I say something?

"Let's go upstairs." He takes my hand with his blood-free one and leads me toward the foyer and then up the two flights of stairs.

When we reach the bedroom, Luca heads straight to

shower. I walk toward the bed, sit down at the edge and wait, my eyes glued to the bathroom door. I've just witnessed a man being slaughtered in front of me, but instead of processing that, I'm freaking out because Luca, obviously, remembers everything.

What happens now? Will he throw me out? Divorce me? I don't think I can live in the same house with him if he goes back to his old self, but just the thought of not being close to him makes me want to scream. The sound of the water stops, and I hold my breath.

The bathroom door opens and Luca steps out, naked. His hair is wet and falling on either side of his face, just like in my first memory of him. I stand up and watch him approach, waiting. When he's right in front of me, he lifts his hand and takes my chin, tilting my head up.

"I'm sorry for lying to you," I whisper.

He bends his head until our noses are barely an inch apart. "About what?"

"About you being in love with me," I choke out.

The corners of Luca's lips curve up. "But you weren't lying, Isabella." His hand leaves my chin to travel down along my neck and chest, then around my waist to the small of my back. "You see, I was already crazy about you, way before the crash."

My breath catches. I open my mouth to say something, but nothing comes out.

"I'm so sorry for being a moron, Isa. For pushing you away, even after I fell in love with you" The arm around my midsection tightens, pressing me against his body. "I was afraid that you were too young."

"You were wrong," I say, while happy tears gather at the

corners of my eyes. I never dared to hope that I'd hear those words leave his lips.

"I know." He presses his lips to mine. "Will you let me show you how sorry I am?"

"Maybe."

Luca's eyes flare. "Maybe?"

I raise my arms to brush my fingers into his wet strands and look straight into his eyes. "You're going to fuck me. First with your mouth. Then your hand. And finally, with your cock."

"All right."

"But, Luca . . ." I squeeze his hair. "You're not allowed to come until you have me absolutely sated."

A wicked smile spreads across his lips, and the next moment, I find myself thrown onto the bed.

"I don't think I've ever told you,"—he says as he crawls up over my body—"how utterly in love I am with your cunning mind."

"Just my mind?" I ask, then gasp when a tearing sound fills the room. "For God's sake, Luca. Stop destroying my clothes."

"I will destroy anything that comes between me and your body." A kiss lands at the side of my neck, then his mouth moves lower, across my collarbone and chest, to my breasts. I reach behind my back and quickly unclasp the bra so it won't also end up destroyed.

Luca's huge hands cup my breasts, squeezing lightly. "I love your pretty boobs." He bites at my left one, then the right. "As well as the rest of your body." He trails kisses down my stomach. "And your greedy little pussy."

He takes the waistband of my panties, and an instant later,

a bundle of torn beige lace lands on the floor. I grip at his hair, panting, as he slowly removes the pussy plug. A moan leaves my lips when he buries his face between my legs and sucks on my clit.

"I've changed my mind, I need your cock, now," I whimper. The need to have it inside me is making me insane. Luca grabs my legs and throws them over his shoulders.

"Not yet." His tongue slides between my folds, and I shudder.

Luca laps at my pussy, switching between licking and sucking as if it's an ice cream, and the pressure between my legs builds until I feel like I'm going to melt from the inside. I arch my back, pulling at the long dark strands between my fingers, pushing his head down even more. My body is already shaking when he starts slowly sliding his finger inside. I come before it's even halfway in.

"You even taste like fucking vanilla, Isa," Luca says as he licks away all my wetness, then lowers my legs and hovers over me. His finger is still inside my pussy, pumping in and out, milking me even more.

"So, you're not mad that I lied?" I whisper against his lips.

"You weren't lying. I already told you,"—he adds another finger, thrusting deeper—"I fell for you way before I lost my memories, tesoro. For your stubborn personality. For the way you stood your ground and fought me every time I acted like an idiot."

"Yes, you did that quite often." I grab his thick arm and ride his fingers.

"I'm sorry." There's a bite on my chin, and another one at the side of my neck. "From now on, I promise I'll treat you like I should have from the start."

"And how would that be?"

His fingers still for a moment, but then he thrusts them inside so hard I gasp. "Like a fucking queen, Isabella."

His words. His fingers. Him. It's too much.

I come again, tears in my eyes and a wide smile on my lips.

Luca's arm encircles me, and he flips me around until I'm on my stomach. "And now, I'm going to royally fuck you. With your magnificent noble ass on display the whole time." He grips my hips, lifts my pelvis, and buries himself inside of me.

I grab at the headboard and hold on with all my might as Luca rocks into me from behind, trying to match my breathing to his tempo. Him, inside—I take a deep breath. Exhale when he slides out. I don't think I'm getting enough air because I'm feeling lightheaded. It could be due to the lack of oxygen or maybe because I'm going to come for the third time in under ten minutes, and my body has trouble processing that. Luca's hand moves between my legs, and his fingers find my clit. He slams into me again, pressing onto my bud at the same time, and white stars burst behind my eyelids. I scream as I come, the sounds mixing with his groans as he explodes into me.

A kiss at the base of my neck, then another one. "Are you asleep?"

I open my eyes and throw a look over my shoulder. "Yes. And I'm half dead, so you can forget about it."

It's been an hour since he destroyed me in the best possible way, and I still can't make myself move.

"Are you sure?" He pushes his finger even deeper inside of me.

"Yes, I'm—"

BANG!

I go stone-still. "Was that a gunshot?"

"Sounds like it." Luca moves his lips to my shoulder.

"Are you not going check what's going on?"

"We have over forty security men on the premises at the moment. Let them earn their paychecks."

Another gunshot rings out somewhere in the garden, and then the sound of male yelling reaches us through the window.

"You piece of shit! I'm going to fucking kill you!"

I look at Luca. "That sounded like Franco."

"Jesus fuck." He shakes his head, reaches for his phone, and calls someone. "Marco, is my brother still alive?"

"He was two minutes ago when he ran out of the house in only his pants. Unbuttoned," Marco's voice comes across the line. "Mr. Conti found him with Miss Arianna in the library."

"Perfect. Should I come down?"

"I think it would be a good idea, Boss."

Luca ends the call and looks down at me. "I'm going downstairs to deal with Franco and shoo the rest of the guests out of our home. I'd hoped they leave after the bloodshed."

"Are you kidding? It'll be the main source of gossip for the next six months."

He slides his hand to my ass and squeezes my butt cheek. "I'll be back in twenty. Then we'll continue."

"Of course, Luca." I smirk.

His eyes flare and he bends his head until his lips touch mine. "I love you, my beautiful, cunning Isa."

Epilogue

Luca

Four years later

My phone on the nightstand rings. I put down the folder I've been holding and pick up the phone with my left hand since my right one is cupping Isabella's pussy, my finger buried inside. And unless there's a fire or something similar, I don't plan on removing it. I look at the screen showing the caller's name and furrow my eyebrows.

"Who is it?" Isabella mumbles sleepily.

"Salvatore Ajello," I say and take the call. "Yes?"

"Mr. Rossi. We may have a problem."

"Something regarding the last construction project?"

"No. This is a personal matter," he says. "There's something of yours here. Something that shouldn't have been in my city, Mr. Rossi."

Jesus fuck. If someone from our Family was crazy enough

to enter the New York region without permission, he's dead, and there's nothing I can do about it.

"Who is it?" I ask.

There are a few moments of silence before he finally answers.

"Milene Scardoni."

The End

Dear reader,

Thanks so much for reading Isabella's and Luca's story! I hope you'll consider leaving a review, letting the other readers know what you thought of Ruined Secrets. Even if it's just one short sentence, it makes a huge difference. Reviews help authors find new readers, and help other readers find new books to love!

If you want to read more of my books, check out my website, or my author page on Amazon, and stay up to date by following me on social media. The next book in the series is **Stolen Touches,** which follows the notorious Salvatore Ajello (the don of the New York branch of Cosa Nostra) and Milene (Bianca's sister, introduced in book two, Broken Whispers). This is an arranged marriage, enemies to lovers, age gap story (Salvatore is 35, Milene is 22).

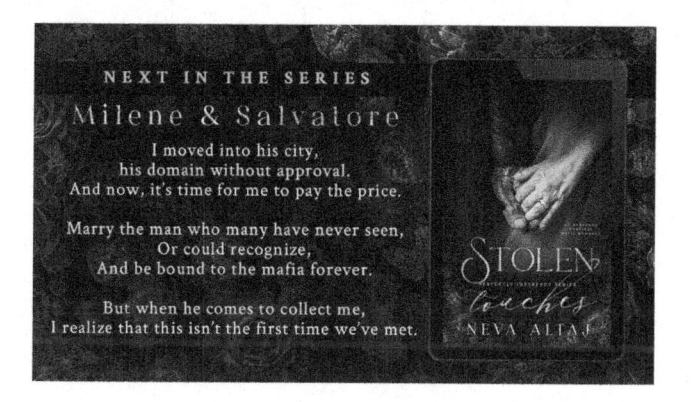

NEXT IN THE SERIES
Milene & Salvatore

I moved into his city,
his domain without approval.
And now, it's time for me to pay the price.

Marry the man who many have never seen,
Or could recognize,
And be bound to the mafia forever.

But when he comes to collect me,
I realize that this isn't the first time we've met.

STOLEN
touches
NEVA ALTAJ

Acknowledgments

One enormous special thank you goes to my personal assistant, Caitlen, whom I can't ever thank enough for her help. I would be so lost without you! Thank you for bearing with me <3

As always, a big thank you to my editor Susan, and my proofreaders—Andie and Yvette, and to my ARC team who caught all the typos and provided great advice for improvement.

And of course, a big thank you to Shaima and Shannon, who beta-read Ruined Secrets and gave amazing guidelines and suggestions for improving the book. Love you babes. <3

A most heartfelt thank you goes out to my readers, who took a chance on a baby author and showed so much love and support, encouraging me to keep writing. Thank you for every review, share, Instagram, and TikTok post because you have no idea how powerful a motivator it is to see that people like your stories.

I love you guys! <3

About the Author

Neva Altaj writes steamy contemporary mafia romance about damaged antiheroes and strong heroines who fall for them. She has a soft spot for crazy jealous, possessive alphas who are willing to burn the world to the ground for their woman. Her stories are full of heat and unexpected turns, and a happily-ever-after is guaranteed every time.

Neva loves to hear from her readers,
so feel free to reach out:

Website: www.neva-altaj.com
Facebook: @neva.altaj
TikTok: @author_neva_altaj
Instagram: @neva_altaj
Amazon Author Page: www.amazon.com/Neva-Altaj
Goodreads: www.goodreads.com/Neva_Altaj

Made in the USA
Monee, IL
03 January 2024